WAKING TERROR

by

Matthew Barron

Published by
Submatter Press

ISBN: 098503887X
ISBN13: 978-0-9850388-7-8

For more information, to contact the author, or to order additional books, visit:
submatterpress.com

A huge thank you to Amber Swartzell and Stacey Deel for their invaluable editing, encouragement and advice.

AN AUTHOR'S NOTE

I first met Jack Mahler (not his real name) at a library author fair in central Indiana. A short, brown ponytail hung out from the white baseball cap which covered his thinning hair. He said he was in town visiting friends. Knowing Jack as I do now, there was probably more to it than that. He had stopped at the table beside mine to look at a book about dogs. I mentioned that I had been "raised by a dog." When Jack looked my way, I added, "My biological parents helped too."

He scanned through my titles and chuckled while we talked about pets. "You write about werewolves and vampires and things?"

"Sometimes," I said. "But I like to put my own spin on them."

"Books and movies never get them right."

That sentence made me just a little apprehensive. Not only was he not buying any books, he seemed ready to go on an insane tangent. But the fair wasn't busy, so I bit. "Are you saying vampires and werewolves are real?"

"Not the way you think, but yeah. I've seen them. They aren't even all that scary compared to what else is out there."

There were still no potential customers nearby, and I loved new ideas for monsters. "What else is there?"

He smirked, but gazed off down the hall. "I've got to get going right now. We'll talk later." With that, he rushed away. Not only had he not gone on a lengthy rant, he had left me wanting more.

I forgot all about the conversation, but a week and a half later I received three small notebooks in the mail full of handwritten notes and one of Jack's business cards. I hadn't given him my address, but he was a private investigator after all. I began deciphering a few pages of chicken scratches and assumed this was his unique way of asking for help writing a fiction book of his own.

Juggling so many projects as well as a day job leaves me little time to help other aspiring authors on their books, no matter how much I might like to, and these notebooks would require extensive work to form into a cohesive, publishable story, but I felt bad that this guy had gone to the trouble of mailing his original notes and worried these were his only copies. My brain started separating the bland, context-less notes into scenes. I decided to give him some general advice and then ask where to mail them back.

When I called him, he insisted the notes were from actual cases he'd worked on and he didn't have any inclination to write a book. I still don't know how much I should believe. Jack is a real PI, and the record of his discharge from the military was easy to find. A few of his notes referenced real people and events I could look up in newspapers, but the articles never mentioned the supernatural.

Over the next few weeks, I went through his notes in more detail, and when something wasn't clear, I called Jack to ask about it. It became obvious this was now more than idle curiosity for me. Jack gave me permission to write his story.

I picked one of the most unbelievable cases to start out with. Jack is pretty convincing and has an answer for every question I ask, but I still tend to be a skeptic. There is certainly some element of truth here, and Jack appears to genuinely believe these stories are real, but I will probably never know for sure where fact and fiction divide.

I separated out what I thought would make the most complete stories, fleshed out scenes and put events in different order for better readability, but I haven't altered the basic content of Jack's original notes.

This is for you, Jack. I hope you like it.

CHAPTER 1

The drive up to Rio Rancho only took about twenty-five minutes once morning rush hour had ended. It was a boring twenty-five minutes, but after all the things I'd seen, boring wasn't so bad. Luis had surprised me by assigning me a routine life insurance claim investigation. All I had to do was verify that the insurance application was accurate and that there was no foul play.

The policy was only ten months old, otherwise there would be no need for an investigation at all. The insured, Alice McGuiness, had died in an automobile accident, her car wrapped around a tree. She was only 33 years old and in good health. Cause of death was pretty obvious, but there was always some sort of verification when the insured died within two years of the policy being initiated. With half a million at stake, the insurance company wanted someone on the ground to physically look things over.

I'd look at some medical records, talk to a couple family members and have the rest of the afternoon to take the dogs on a hike in the Sandias. It sounded easy enough, but Net Life was a big client. Luis wanted to make them happy, and he didn't exactly trust me to be professional. Fortunately for me, any of the investigators who had come through the Navarro Investigations office last week during the White Witch incident were still out sick, and none of the other PIs Luis farmed work to seemed interested.

I pulled the rented SUV to the curb. My old wagon was in the shop more than it was on the road these days, but I'd have the money for something better soon.

The person to identify Mrs. McGuiness' body was her husband, Stephen, also the beneficiary of all that money. The McGuiness couple lived in a nice subdivision in a two story house. The yard wasn't green like the lawns I had grown up with. Instead, a bed of pebbles and some trimmed shrubbery surrounded the house. The Sandia Mountains loomed fifteen miles to the east, while everything in Rio Rancho was flat, nothing around me but houses sprouting from the desert.

I wore a khaki sport coat when I wanted to look a little professional. I didn't need a gun for this job, but the weight of the pistol strapped under the jacket gave a sense of security. The Beretta subcompact operated like the M9 I had trained with in the army, just a little smaller. Luis wanted me to cut my hair, but it looked classy enough when tied back, even if it was a little thin on top. It came just past my shoulders— like I said, classy enough. I wasn't in the military anymore, and I'd be damned before I buzzed my hair again.

Maybe damned wasn't the best word. I knew better than most how literal damned could be.

I rang the bell and waited. I had to ring it two more times before a strapping young man in a white polo shirt finally opened the door. Mr. Stephen McGuiness stood a full head taller than me with trimmed blond hair and blue eyes. At twenty-seven, Stephen was seven years younger than me, worked in security, owned this nice house, and, until last week, had a lovely wife.

This could have been my life if I hadn't taken some dark detours. I'd fallen in with a very bad crowd, some scary people I hoped never to meet again.

Dark circles under Stevie's eyes marred his god-like appearance. He smelled of unwashed sweat.

"Mr. McGuiness, my name is Jack Mahler. Net Life sent me to confirm a few details regarding your wife's insurance policy."

He stood still and stoic. "Is there a problem?"

"Not at all. This is just routine."

He stared at me from the doorway.

"May I come in?"

He looked at the darkened living room behind him and hesitated, but then motioned inside. The curtains were drawn and the harsh New Mexico sun barely made a dent in the musty gloom. My foot crunched over scattered papers and I stepped around a broken coffee mug. The furniture was still in place, but the shelves were empty and the walls blank. Picture frames and cooking pots littered the floor. Broken plates and miscellaneous papers fell randomly about the room.

"Tornado hit this place?" I said.

He rubbed his left arm and looked at the mess around us. "Too many memories here. Guess I took out my frustrations." A sudden bitterness entered his voice. "You know my wife died, right? Isn't that why you are here?"

I was surprised by the vitriol, but I suppose I shouldn't have been. All the things a person has to deal with when a loved one dies, and then I walk in questioning the life insurance policy. "I hate to bother you at this difficult time, but the sooner we get this out of the way, the sooner your claim will be paid out. It's just a formality, really."

"Yeah. Okay." He cleared a box off the couch and we sat down.

A whiff of sulfur entered my nostrils, reminding me of the parking lot at the shooting range. The stairs by the door creaked. "Is there someone else here?" I asked.

"Just me. I'm all alone now."

The tired grief in his response made me uncomfortable. No one likes to talk about death. I ignored the answer and started in with my questions.

"How did you meet your wife?" I asked.

"I found her on Match Date four years ago. We hit it off right away. It was like we were made for each other." There was something rehearsed in the way he said it, like he was reading from cue cards. Being low on sleep could produce that detached effect.

"I thought you worked for Mrs. McGuiness' dad."

His face flushed red. "Not *for* her dad. I worked security in the same building. He helped me get the job *after* me and Alice got engaged. Alice and I were perfect for each other. Our Match Date profiles couldn't have been closer if we had designed them that way."

I wasn't sure why he was getting defensive, but I tried to change tracks. I picked up a broken picture frame on the floor next to the couch. Through the cracked glass was an image of a plain girl with bobbed, dirty-blonde hair. Her red dress peeked from behind Stevie. She had her arm around him and a wide, genuine smile.

"She looks very happy with you."

Stevie took the picture and sank into the couch. "She was."

"Was she in good health?" I'd seen her charts, and already knew she was healthy, but I needed to reboot this interview. Plus, sometimes interviewees will inadvertently add new information that wasn't in the charts or the insurance application.

"She was in good shape. No medical issues if that's what you want to know."

"Nothing new to report since the life insurance application was filed?"

"No."

"Where was she driving to the night she died?"

"She was planning to make lasagna for dinner. She was mad because I was supposed to buy ricotta cheese on my way home from work. If I'd just remembered to stop at the store, maybe she would still be alive."

Again, it sounded rehearsed. I couldn't get a read on this guy. The way he sank when I mentioned how happy she looked— he must have cared about her, but the rest of the time, he sounded disingenuous.

I guess I was expected to offer some sympathetic platitude. "It wasn't your fault. You couldn't have known."

He gazed at the picture in his hand.

The smell of sulfur remained faint, but unmistakable. "Do you own a gun?" I asked.

His eyes shot upward at my sudden tangent. "I work security. Of course I own a gun."

"Have you ever fired it inside the house?"

"No. Is that a standard question?"

I gave the most sincere smile I could fake. "Just curious. I had a rat in my apartment the other day. Took out my Px Storm and went after it. The neighbors weren't too happy with me."

His brow furrowed. "What does this have to do with the insurance policy?"

The ceiling creaked above our heads. "You're sure no one else is here?"

"The house does that from time to time. All the temperature changes out here."

I nodded. "I think I have all I need for now. May I use your restroom before I leave? I have a long drive back to the office."

His jaw clenched. "I suppose."

I smiled again, and he directed me up the stairs. The bathroom smelled of ammonia and aftershave. An empty roll of toilet paper remained in the dispenser while a half-used roll sat on the back of the toilet. The toilet seat was up, and spots of dry urine decked the rim. Evidently Stevie wasn't the clean one in the marriage.

I opened up the medicine cabinet and found the traditional things one would expect to find: bandages, ointment, toothpaste, aspirin. Mrs. McGuiness had allergy pills and two prescriptions, flunitrazepam and galantamine *for the treatment of sleeplessness.*

Sleep aids weren't listed on the insurance application. I pictured Alice's head lolling as she drove. There were no skid marks mentioned in the police report. She hadn't braked. The prescription was only two months old though, so they wouldn't have been listed on the application and probably weren't significant enough to warrant a change. I took a pic of the bottles with my phone, made a note of the doctor's name and quietly went back into the hallway.

No one else would have picked up the smell of gunpowder, but I traced it to an open doorway. The bedroom was a mess just like the living room. Bed sheets tangled with the blanket on the bed. Drawers lay half open or sat inverted on the opposite side of the room. A closet door hung from one hinge.

A bullet blemished the smooth drywall across from the foot of the bed. It was fresh, probably fired last night. It was odd, but technically not illegal, and his wife had died a week ago, not last night. This had no direct bearing on her death, although it did say something about Stevie's temperament. Mr. McGuiness was not playing with a full deck, and I certainly wouldn't buy a used car from him.

The voice startled me. "Nightmares." Stevie stood in the bedroom entrance. He looked annoyed but must have felt he needed to give some explanation. "I've been having nightmares since Alice was… since she died." He forced a smile. "I guess I shouldn't keep my gun next to the bed."

I raised my eyebrows. "Must have been some nightmare!"

He rubbed his arm again, and fondled the wedding band on his left hand. "It was." Light glinted off another ring, a silver one, on his right index finger.

"You should probably talk to someone. You've suffered a terrible loss. There's no shame in seeking help."

He stiffened, his guard up once more. "I'm already seeing a doctor. Are we done?"

I nodded and headed downstairs. "I'll call if I have any more questions."

"When will I receive my check?"

"I'll give my report to Net Life and they will review it. Probably no more than a couple of weeks."

He scowled at that.

"Could be as soon as a day or two though. Thank you for your time," I said as he closed the door behind me.

I went back out to the rented SUV. At this time during a weekday, the driveways were empty, homeowners all at work.

A breeze seemed to ruffle curtains in a window across the street, but the window was closed. The air conditioner hummed.

I took a look back at the McGuiness house before marching up to the residence across the street. I had barely touched the doorbell when the front door cracked open. A papery face peeked under the chain. The old woman motioned her chin across the street and asked, "You a friend of Steve McGuiness?"

"No," I said. "My name's Jack Mahler. I work for Net Life. I'm just asking a few questions about Mrs. McGuiness."

"Oh." The old woman flung the door wide. She wore a floral printed house dress and walked with a rickety walker. Her head came up to my chest and she slouched in a way that made her back look like a hump. "That sweet girl! We usually have brunch on Tuesdays, but she didn't come by this week. Is she okay?"

I was stunned. "You don't know?"

She brought her hand to her mouth. "Did something happen? Is she hurt?"

"I'm sorry to be the one to tell you, but… Alice died in a car accident early last week."

She clenched her hands around the walker and scowled up at me. "You must be mistaken! I heard them fighting again last night."

"I'm afraid it's true. I've seen the accident report and the death certificate. What do you mean fighting?"

"Oh, they've had some doozies, but this week's been really bad." She lowered her voice and leaned in, even though there was no one else around to hear. "I heard them throwing dishes at each other."

"Did Mrs. McGuiness ever have bruises or black eyes?"

The old woman shook her head. "It was never like that. She gave as good as she got. In fact, I think she usually started it."

"Did you notice a lot of family coming by after the funeral? Cars in the driveway?"

"No. They were a solitary couple. Alice didn't have many friends. Why else would that lovely young girl spend her Tuesdays with an old lady like me?"

"Was she acting strangely the last time you saw her?"

"No… Well…"

"What?"

"I think she may have developed a drinking problem. It's not my place to judge, but the last few times she was here, she was slurring her words."

Prescription sleep aids and alcohol, I thought. *A bad combination for driving.* "What about last night during the fight? Was there a car in the driveway?"

A mischievous smile grew across her face. "You think Steve was having an affair? Not in that house he wasn't. I know everything that goes on in this neighborhood. Now, Mrs. Henderson in the house next to them, that's a different story. She has a landscaper come by twice a week. Grass doesn't grow that fast here! No one needs a landscaper to come twice a week!"

"Well, you don't know everything that goes on here. Alice died a week ago." I really need to work on my tact. No wonder Luis doesn't trust me to talk to clients.

She slapped her walker against the floor tiles. "I'm telling you she ain't dead! If she was, I'd know it! I don't know why you're playing this cruel joke and I don't care! You get out of here!"

"So no one has been visiting Mr. McGuiness?"

Her paper-white face flushed red. She slammed the door, and the deadbolt clicked into place.

I pulled out a business card and left it in the crack between the door and the frame. "Call me if you think of anything," I shouted.

I turned back to the SUV and saw the blind at the McGuiness house fall quickly back into place.

The McGuiness couple wasn't as perfect as Stevie wanted them to appear, but they certainly weren't fighting last night. Even if he was having an affair, it didn't necessarily invalidate the life insurance policy. It wasn't my job to dig up all of Stevie's dirt, just to make sure Alice's death was an accident.

I grabbed the laptop from under the seat in the SUV and typed in the address of the old woman I'd just spoken to. Her name was Abigail Duncan, a widow. As nosey as Abby was, how did she not know about Alice? I opened up the Albuquerque Journal in my browser and scanned the obituaries. One sentence was all Alice got, the standard copy sent from the coroner. While other people had full paragraphs and photos devoted to them, no one had bothered to do anything extra for Alice. A flash of anger passed over me. It was unimaginable Stevie wouldn't tell Alice's friend and neighbor she had died! Abby hadn't yet accepted that her friend was dead, but she would. That's why she was really so angry. The reality was sinking in.

I now realized why none of the other investigators wanted this assignment. Cheating spouses and missing persons might be sleazy or more complicated, but talking to people about their recently dead loved ones wasn't as simple as I had thought.

I'd already written a first draft of my report for Net Life. I had used a template and filled out the information from the application and the coroner's report. I thought by now I'd be making minor alterations and sending the report to Luis to go over before he sent it on to Net Life. I'd have the rest of the day off. Quick and simple. But there were a few too many oddities, and I wanted to do just a tiny bit more checking before sending my report on its way.

I opened my dummy Facebook account. I didn't understand the appeal of living all your life in a box or on a phone. The world around me was much more interesting, but social media was an essential tool of my trade. I didn't need to hunt for private information when people put it all out there for me. I used an alias on social networks because there were some people I didn't want to know I was still alive.

Some very dangerous people.

It had taken me eleven years to claw my way back from what Catalyst had done to me. I hadn't heard any mention about the techno-cult or their perverse experiments since returning to civilization, and that was fine with me. I didn't think they could possibly still be around after eleven years, but I wasn't about to go looking. Survivalist militias had a way of surviving.

There were also people back in Indiana who still assumed I was dead. I didn't want them finding out I was alive in some random Facebook post, yet I didn't care enough to go back and see them in person either. With Mom gone, there was nothing left in Indiana for me, no reason to go back.

I indulged a self-punishing whim and clicked through images of the one person in Indiana I still gave a crap about. Jessie, my high school girlfriend, posed happily with her husband in her profile picture. Two beautiful kids dominated her photos. The son posed with a ball in his soccer uniform. He had won a trophy in the science fair because his egg survived a three story fall in the contraption he had built. The daughter was a princess for Halloween, but in another shot she was covered in grease while helping her dad fix the car. Jessie's life had moved on without me.

I clicked out of her profile and searched for Alice McGuiness. It was pointless to dwell on what might have been. I wouldn't have wanted Jessie to wait for me. No woman should wait nine years for a guy. She was happy, and I was happy for her.

Alice McGuiness had thirty-five online friends, mostly people she knew from high school. Most of her posts involved cats doing cute things. She posted her wedding album and a few pictures of her and Stevie. Other than the wedding photos, she was always wearing the same red dress. Five of her thirty-five friends wished her a happy birthday last month, but I doubted any of them had spoken to her in real life since graduation.

I flipped open my phone and Diane's nasally voice answered, "Yes, I took the dogs out on my way into the office."

"Do I only call you to check on the dogs?"

"Did you call just to say hi?"

"Maybe."

"What do you want, Jack?"

"Can you look up Alice McGuiness' father for me? He was the only other family member listed."

"You have your laptop and database access. You can do it just as easily as I can."

"But you do it so much better."

She released a long, tired breath.

"I'm sorry," I said. "I just… I need to hear a friendly voice. I don't know why I never considered how difficult this could be. I'm talking to people about the tragic death of their friend and wife. I was looking at this as a report I needed to finish, a piece of paper, but Alice McGuiness was a human being."

I could almost hear the smile in Diane's voice. "Oh Jack, you're kind of stupid and sweet at the same time. It really never occurred to you that this woman was real?"

My face reddened with shame. "Well, I mean, I knew that on some level, but I guess I was thinking more about my report." And about my afternoon off, but I didn't want to admit that to Diane at that moment.

"In our line of work, a little detachment is a necessity, but we can't forget these are people."

"Maybe you should tell that to your boss," I said.

Diane Bowen was Luis' office manager. She answered the phones, took care of the accounting, and paid the PIs. She didn't have a detective's license, but she'd been with Luis long enough to pick up many technical aspects of the job and probably knew more tricks of the trade than I did.

You might be thinking either Luis or me or perhaps both of us are sexist pigs for rushing me through to get my license while Diane answers phones. Actually, while I made a nice chunk of money after a case, Diane ran all the day-to-day business of the agency. She made more money per year than me, and it was steady money, while I got paid per job. I didn't have the education or the mind for numbers she did. I didn't like to think of Diane as my boss, that was Luis, but she had a lot of say in how cases were assigned and she did sign my paychecks, so…

I was lucky she took an interest in my well-being. She probably saw me as a charity case. I'd literally walked into town with nothing, and I doubt I could have made it as far as I had without her assistance behind the scenes.

Luis hadn't exactly been thrilled about helping me get my license either. He wasn't normally the mentor type. I kind of, well, sort of blackmailed him into helping me.

Every PI in town does work for Luis Navarro from time to time. Even the ones who don't work directly for him stay in business because Luis farms out work to us. When I wandered into town two and a half years ago, I stumbled upon a missing kid in a high profile case. Luis took the credit by saying I worked for him. I stayed silent, and he helped me get my license. He actually got my military time to count as experience even though I'd been kicked out. While we didn't always get along, he made good on our deal, and I had to give him credit for that.

But that's a whole other story.

Diane tapped keys on the other end of the phone. "I'm emailing the contact information for Albert Ellison, Alice McGuiness' father."

"Thanks, Diane. Oh and Diane…"

"Yes?" she said expectantly.

"Can you check on the dogs again tonight? I'm going to be up here later than I thought."

"I'll do it, Jack, but for the dogs, not for you."

"Thanks, Diane. You're a true friend."

"I know," she said. "I'm a pal." She clicked off.

Since returning to civilization, Diane had been my most consistent friend. She was the only human I truly trusted, but there were things I couldn't tell anyone, even her.

CHAPTER 2

I passed a field of shiny solar panels and pulled into the Sandia Research Park visitor lot. The gentle hum of the substation across the street was drowned out by an F16 roaring in for a landing at Kirtland Air Force base.

Behind a Plexiglas wall on the left-hand side of the reception area, an overweight man in blue chewed on a meatball sub and looked over a clipboard. I hadn't eaten breakfast, and the aromatic garlic and oregano made my stomach growl. He was a far cry from the trim Stevie McGuiness. His nametag read *Michael*. Barely visible from my angle was a large monitor partitioned with views of all the entranceways.

I tapped on the Plexiglas. "I'm here to see Dr. Albert Ellison."

The guard wiped marinara from his chin. "Is he expecting you?"

"Nope," I said. "He isn't answering either of his phones. I need to speak to him about his daughter."

The guard gave a longing look at the sandwich and picked up the phone. "Dr. Ellison. There's a gentleman here to see you. Says it's about your daughter."

The guard eyed me suspiciously and hung up the phone. "He'll be down in a minute."

"Thanks."

I circled five uncomfortable looking chairs and a way too cushy couch in the reception area. Pacing wasn't professional, so I tried sitting in one of the stiff-backed chairs. My right leg shook involuntarily. I'd spent too much time on my ass. My leg stopped quaking when I looked at it or thought about it, and the guard was ignoring me, but it made me feel out of control and unprofessional.

I stood and tapped on the Plexiglas again. "Say, you wouldn't know Stevie McGuiness by any chance?"

"Steve? He used to work here. Why?"

"Used to? Did he quit?"

"He quit after his wife died."

My voice dropped. "Dr. Ellison's daughter."

"What about her?"

"Stevie's wife was Dr. Ellison's daughter."

Mikey furrowed his brow. "I don't think so. Was she? You sure you're here to see the right person?"

"I thought I was. How well did you know Stevie?"

Mikey shrugged his shoulders. "I don't know. As well as anyone, I guess."

I leaned against the Plexiglas. "You know, you and I are practically in the same field. Before I became an investigator, I tried to get into private security, but no one was hiring."

His attitude changed a little. "Security's a lot of responsibility. Not just anyone can do this. I always thought I'd be a good private eye. I've got a mind for details."

"I bet you do. What can you tell me about Stevie?"

Mikey shrugged again. "Not much."

I tried not to sigh with exasperation. *Mind for details,* indeed. "Was he good at his job?"

Mikey rolled his eyes. "I'll say."

"Being good at your job is a bad thing?"

"He was a nice enough guy, but just a little *too* good, if you know what I mean. He made the rest of us look bad." Mikey raised his voice, evidently imitating someone in authority, "*Stephen* never eats at *his* desk." He shook his head and explained, "I'm hypoglycemic. If I don't eat often enough, I could die!"

"That sounds serious!"

He conjured the imitated voice again. "Michael, why didn't you make your rounds yet. Stephen always makes his rounds on schedule." Mikey waved his hand in the air and let it drop back to the desk. "Things have been a little more relaxed since Steve left." As if to illustrate the point, Mikey took a huge bite of his sandwich.

A man in a green sweater vest over an ochre dress shirt pushed open the glass door. A crescent of blond hair rimmed his bald head, and a trim goatee and mustache grew under his nose and glasses. "You have something to say about my daughter?" He wasn't wearing any cologne, only mild antiperspirant. It was refreshing to find someone not covered in volatile scents.

I smiled and extended my hand. "My name's Jack Mahler. I work for Net Life. I'm just asking a few standard questions regarding the life insurance policy on your daughter. You knew Stephen had a life insurance policy on her?"

Dr. Ellison hesitantly took my hand. His grip was gentle and his hand smooth. "Not specifically, but it is logical to assume they would both have policies." He cast a glance at Mikey and opened the door wider. "Come along back."

"Not so fast," Mikey said. "You're going to need to fill out a form if you're going inside."

I filled out a form stating my name, company, and who I was visiting. Then I handed over my driver's license for Mikey to hold at the desk. In return, he gave me a visitor's badge to clip on my jacket.

"Do you have a phone?" Mikey asked.

"Of course."

"I'm going to have to keep that too."

I protested, "I use my phone for business!"

"Phones have cameras on them," Mikey said. "We can't have anyone taking pictures inside the facility. You understand, one professional to another."

Mikey winked, and I handed over my phone. I was glad I'd had the foresight to leave my gun in the SUV. I didn't think it was a good idea to bring it into a federal lab, even with my permit, and it turned out I was right.

I followed Dr. Ellison down the hall, and we huffed up the stairs to the second floor. "It's faster than the elevator," he said.

"I wasn't expecting so much security," I said.

"There are a few sensitive projects going on here. Last year there was an attempt to steal the prototype I'm working on."

Dr. Ellison's office was cluttered with papers and diagrams. Two large monitors sat on his desk.

"What are you working on?" I said. "Am I allowed to ask?"

Ellison gave me a faint smile. "Of course. I'm working on a matter anti-matter cell, the Dynamo Capsule, small enough to fit in your hand. One capsule could, theoretically, power an entire city. If we can make it work safely, it will solve the energy crisis."

"Wow!" I said. "That would be revolutionary— reshape the world economy and national security."

His smile broadened for a moment. "Indeed. But you didn't come here to talk about my work."

I nodded. "No. I'm sorry. I need to ask a few questions before Net Life can pay out the claim."

He nodded and his expression darkened. "I understand."

"Did your daughter have any health conditions?"

"No. Not that I am aware of," he said. "But she died in a car accident, I don't see what that would have to do with anything."

"Just a standard question. Was she on any anxiety meds or meds to help her sleep?"

"Not that I know of."

"How well did you know Stevie, her husband."

He beamed. "Ah, Stephen is a good lad! A gentleman! Thorough. Bright. He asks about my work, and, at least on a layman's level, really seems to grasp what my team is doing. I was so happy Alice found a man like him to take care of her."

"Did she need taking care of?"

"What do you mean?"

"She didn't work, seldom left the house, but they didn't have any kids. In this day and age, that is a bit unusual."

"Stephen is old fashioned. He believes a man should take care of his wife. They were planning on having children someday."

"So it was a good marriage? They never fought?"

"All couples fight. Alice…" He cocked his head "…could be difficult. But Stephen was patient, almost to a fault. They were seeing a counselor."

I hadn't found any insurance claims for a counselor or a therapist, but not all therapists billed insurance. "Do you remember the name of the counselor?"

"Ah, no," he said. "But I know a couple of scientists here see the same one. I can get the name for you."

"That would be great. I'm surprised to find you back at work so soon."

"I'm afraid I wouldn't be much use to Alice or Stephen now. It's too late for me to help my daughter," he said. "The lead on my project left after the incident last year. I've got to create a secure containment field for the capsule, or the whole project is useless. It is all riding on me now."

"It almost sounds like you were closer to Stephen than you were to your daughter."

Ellison's eyes sank to the papers covering his desk. "Alice and I always had trouble relating to each other. My wife died when Alice was nineteen. Maude was the parent. As a child, Alice was ready for bed by the time I got home from work. Alice dropped out of college after Maude passed. She was lost, and nothing I did or said helped. I was so happy when Stephen began courting her. She finally had someone to look after her, and I could concentrate on my work." He gazed past me with a faint smile. "Stephen and I could talk for hours about my projects. He even became a sounding board for my ideas."

I hadn't heard the word *courting* in quite a while. Dr. Ellison seemed perfectly happy to hand his daughter off so he could avoid dealing with her.

"Were you upset that Stephen quit his job here?"

"He quit?"

"According to Mikey."

"Mikey?"

"Michael, the guard out front. The one who took my phone."

I was surprised how little people knew about each other here.

"I didn't know. Perhaps I should call Stephen."

"Maybe you should." There was judgment in my voice, very unprofessional. "Stevie seemed very distraught when I spoke to him earlier today. Did he have a temper?"

"Stephen? No. Not at all. He was so patient! Alice was the hothead. She didn't know how to relate to men. I blame myself. She didn't have a male influence growing up. I was so relieved when Stephen came along. If I could go back and change things, I would have spent more time with Alice and Maude. There was always some big new discovery, some project mere steps from completion. But it's too late." He tapped the monitors. "This is all there is now."

"I'm sorry."

Ellison took off his glasses and rubbed his eyes. "No, I'm sorry. I'm under a lot of pressure."

"Can you get me the name of that therapist?" I wanted to recommend Dr. Ellison see the therapist too, but I'd already overstepped my boundaries.

"Hold on one moment," he said.

Dr. Ellison left the room. I took a peek at the computer screens. The computer had clicked out of screen saver mode when he tapped the monitor. On the left screen was a series of equations with letters and numbers completely indecipherable to me. On the other was a diagram with two circles surrounded by dotted lines. I heard footsteps beyond the open door and retook my seat.

Ellison handed me a business card.

"Dr. David Brown," I read. The same name on Alice's pill bottles.

Dr. Ellison walked me back down to security.

"I may have some follow up questions," I said. "I want to make sure all the *i*'s are dotted and the *t*'s crossed so the claim will be processed and paid as quickly as possible. Do you ever answer your phone?" That last question came out ruder than I intended. I tried to back track. "When is the best time to call?"

"I'll try to be more responsive."

"Thanks."

Dr. Ellison returned to his office. A different man sat at the security desk now, but the oregano from Mikey's sandwich still permeated the air. The guard handed me the clip board to sign out.

"Did you know Stevie McGuiness?" I asked.

"Of course! Great guy! You know him?"

"We're buddies," I said.

"Steve covered my shift so I could visit my brother when my niece was born. He was always doing stuff for people like that. Some weeks, he practically lived here."

"That's good ol' Steve," I said. "As long as you don't get on his bad side. Quite a temper on that guy."

"Really? I didn't know that. He was always pleasant at work."

I retrieved my phone and license and walked back out to the visitor lot.

So, Stevie was likeable, a model employee, the perfect son-in-law, never lost his temper, but his house was trashed and there was a bullet in his bedroom wall.

I had missed a call while I was in with Doc Ellison. Nobody spoke on the short voicemail, just silence before they hung up. I called back. After four rings, I heard a click, and old Abby's muffled voice whirred along an old, cassette style answering machine. "I can't come to the phone right now..." I hadn't heard one of those in quite a while. Everyone had digital voicemail these days.

"This is Jack Mahler," I said. "I saw you called when I was in a meeting. I'm available now. If I don't hear from you, I'll try again later."

My stomach growled. It was way past lunchtime. As much as I hated to, I'd need to return the rental and reclaim my junker before thinking about food.

***

Spike's white hair contrasted coal-black skin. Curly hair glistened with sweat, and grease speckled his coveralls. He handed me the bill for replacing the head gasket on my 1992 Ford Escort station wagon.

I shook my head and let out a long sigh. Spike gave me half the going rate on labor, but it was still a big hit to my new car fund. "The wagon is on its last legs. Soon, I'll have enough money for a down payment on something better."

Spike tapped the fender. '92 Escorts still had that boxy looking front end. Years of sun exposure had discolored the forest green paint on the roof and hood, giving it a spotty, matte finish. Tiny pock marks, hail damage, marred the metal. A jagged hole in the rear wheel well looked like someone had taken a bite out of the metal, and rust along the torn edge revealed the car must have been driven in a colder climate at some point in its long life.

"The old girl's got a lot of life left," Spike said. "You keep bringing her in, I'll keep her running."

I looked at the bill in my hand. "I bet you will."

Spike laughed. I couldn't fault him. If not for Spike, I never would have gotten the car running in the first place, and I needed a car to do my job. Two and a half years ago, I wandered into town on foot with absolutely nothing. This car and Spike's automotive genius gave me a chance at living again.

"Thanks, Spike," I said. "You're a miracle worker."

Spike beamed, showing five big gaps in his teeth. "You're my best customer, Jack."

After the smooth start of the rental, the wagon's grinding ignition sounded horrendous. New car air freshener gave way to burning oil and hot vinyl seats. The AC didn't work, but the windows were already down. I sped up to create a breeze of dusty, dry air, and with it, the smells of the world around me came rushing in. Fryer grease congealed in a recycling bin behind a fast food place. Animal urine marked a tree at the corner. A squirrel decomposed on the side of the road two blocks away.

Lettuce rotted in the trash behind Mr. Dan's Sandwich shop. I hadn't eaten there before but decided to give it a try. I'd heard they had meatball subs.

CHAPTER 3

The sun sank below the horizon as I pulled the wagon into the McGuiness' subdivision. Cars lined the driveways, and houses glowed with electric light. I could clearly see a family sitting down to dinner through a big window. They appeared so vulnerable eating with the curtains open. Anyone driving by could see them. They never considered how easy it would be for any passerby to bust through the glass and destroy their happiness forever. It must be pleasant to feel so safe.

I parked in front of old Abby's house. Stevie wouldn't recognize the wagon. I could sit here and watch as long as I needed to, but the McGuiness house sat completely dark. One dim light emanated through a window from somewhere within Abby's home.

The old woman still hadn't returned my call. I rang her bell and waited. The barely perceptible musk of men's aftershave hung over her doorway. It takes time for a woman with a walker to get around, so I continued to wait. It wasn't late, but perhaps she went to bed early. I flipped out my phone and called. She must have had the volume way up on the ringer. I could hear her phone clearly through the locked door. The answering machine clicked on, and I hung up.

The McGuiness house across the street remained dark.

I went around to the back of Abby's house and peeked into the sliding doors. A nightlight cast shadows over the kitchen. On the floor next to the bar, the old woman's walker lay on its side. I tapped the glass. "Mrs. Duncan!" I shouted. "Mrs. Duncan!"

A broom handle wedged the bottom of the sliding doors shut. I thought about breaking the glass. I'd make quite a mess getting in that way. "Hold on!" I said.

I went to a back door and took the lock pick from my inside jacket pocket. I stuck the tension wrench into the keyhole and gave a gentle turn before inserting the pick. Luis had taught me how to do this and then told me never to do it. I could lose my PI license for breaking and entering or disturbing a crime scene, but this was an exception. Abby could still be alive.

I gently felt for the tumblers with the pick. All but one of them gave, but then I bumped the wrench and they fell back into place.

"Damn!"

I was about to give up and smash the window, but decided to give it one more try. The tumblers clicked, and the knob turned.

I wanted to run into the kitchen, but I restrained myself. It was dark, and I didn't know what I was walking into. "Mrs. Duncan?"

A thick ankle and slippers extended from behind the bar. A cloud of cheap aftershave hung over her lifeless body. There were no marks on her that I could see, but the walker lay off to the side. There was no way she could have been using it for support when she fell.

I thought about leaving. No one knew I'd been there. I didn't want the hassle of dealing with cops or the extra attention. I wondered if I left how long it would be before anyone found her. How long would it take for someone to notice the nosey little neighbor wasn't being nosey anymore?

She deserved better.

I called Allen Deschene. He was the only cop I trusted. He had saved my life once and didn't even know it.

"Yellow," he said. That's how he said hello.

My voice always got a little quieter when I spoke to him. "Allen, it's Jack, Jack Mahler."

"Yeah. What can I do for you, Jack?"

I stuttered and stammered for a moment. "An old woman named Abigail Duncan called me earlier today. I stopped by her place to talk and found her dead."

"Oh... Natural causes?"

I hesitated. Aftershave is not evidence of foul play. The walker being out of position was suspicious, but Allen wouldn't see it that way. "I'm not so sure, but there are no marks that I can see."

"You could have called the desk with this."

"I know. I guess. I just…"

"It's fine. Text me the address. I'll call it in."

"Thanks, Allen," I said. I flipped on the light and looked over the old woman.

I'd have to make a statement, which I didn't want to do, but it was the safest course. If the authorities did find signs of foul play, something I missed, they'd find my business card and hear my messages on her machine. Neighbors might have seen my car in front of her house. I'd be the first suspect. As long as I stayed and answered their questions, I had nothing to worry about. I had good reason for being here, and good reason for breaking in to check on her.

If I was smart, I'd just hold tight and wait for the cops.

I'm not that smart. Unless there was a police car nearby, the cops wouldn't be there for at least fifteen minutes, not for someone who was already dead. I hadn't mentioned any of my suspicions over the phone because I didn't have any evidence to back them up. There was no reason for the police to hurry.

I marched across the street to Stevie's darkened house. The same aftershave in Abby's kitchen hung in his doorway, but it wasn't alone. Sweat from at least four other men lingered by the door. I rang the bell, and then slammed my fist against the door.

I took a deep breath. I had to get control of myself. The house remained dark, no movement within. I took my lock picks back out and went to work.

Okay, this was illegal. This could get my license revoked, and there was a cop on the way too. I already said I wasn't smart, right?

I crept into the house and scanned the floor for debris to step around. When I had been there earlier, there had been papers, broken plates, all kinds of crap. Now there was nothing. Even the furniture was gone! It didn't seem possible it could have all all been packed away and moved so quickly. The floor would just need a good vacuuming and then the house would be ready to go on the market. The kitchen was the same way— no plates or dishes or pots or pans.

I marched up to the bathroom. It still stank of ammonia, and the toilet was still decked with yellow spots, but the medicine cabinet, closet and drawers were all empty. I could smell Stevie's potent aftershave concentrated in the air, but it wasn't the same aftershave from Abby's or the doorway.

Fresh paint overpowered every other smell upstairs.

In the bedroom, the bed and dresser were missing, as I expected. The wall where the bullet had been was now smooth, and the paint over it reflected moonlight from the window. It wasn't a great patch job, but by tomorrow, if they matched the color well enough, no one would know about the bullet.

A flash of red movement caught my eye, and I whirled around, reaching for my holster.

A woman in a red dress stood with her back to me. Her head drooped downward, nose pointing where the bed had been. I slowly brought my hand away from my gun.

My heart thundered in my chest. The house was dead silent, yet I hadn't heard her come in. If she reported me, I was finished.

"Hello," I said.

She had to know I was there, but she remained frozen, staring into space with sunken eyes and downturned lips. Her dress seemed redder than it should be in the dark, almost like it glowed. Her hair tapered down the back of her neck in a bobbed style.

I assumed the darkness was playing tricks on my eyes. I whipped to her side and looked into her face. "Alice?" I said. Perhaps this was a sister or cousin who looked so much like the dead woman.

Her face slowly turned to me, and the window rattled in its frame. Her mournful expression altered by degrees into one of rage. The closet door, already loose, slammed shut and then sprang open again. Moonlight from the window passed through Alice's face and glowed behind her eye.

I sucked in a breath and backed away from the apparition while the closet door continued to bang against the wall. "I'm here to help," I said. "What happened to you?"

She glided closer. Her red dress hung from her torso as though there were no legs underneath. Her eyes gleamed with fury and hatred, and at that moment, it was all directed at me.

The closet door snapped from the hinge and flew across the room, whooshing by my head and bouncing against the wall.

I got out of there.

I tripped running down the stairs in the dark and tumbled down. Sharp corners were blunted by carpet but still hurt as they jabbed into my back.

Strangely, the sudden impact helped calm me down. I lay on the stairs for a moment, catching my breath and trying to think of some reasonable explanation for what I had seen. It's not that I didn't believe ghosts were possible— I'd seen some pretty strange things— but I'd never seen a real ghost before. What other explanation could there be?

I stood slowly, making sure no bones were broken. Moonlight streamed through the open front door below. I took another look up the stairs of the silent house.

A cold draft moved through my bones, and the door slammed shut. There she was, Alice's ghost, the lady in red, blocking my exit. I couldn't see any recognition or intelligence in her eyes, only hatred.

I lifted my hands in submission. "Mrs. McGuiness," I said. "I'm not your enemy."

Her red dress billowed behind her as though sucked by a great wind. She glanced behind her. Scowling eyes widened with sudden terror, and her mouth stretched into a soundless shriek. She reached out to me as though silently pleading. I extended my arm, but my fingers slipped through her immaterial hand. She pulled away from me toward the wooden front door. The entrance was only a few feet from her, but she continued to shrink as though moving a great distance. Her body collapsed into a sparkling glow and was caught in someone's hand.

The wiry man existed behind the grain of the wood door, as though the solid surface were a mesh screen. Angular bones almost protruded from his naked chest. A short, green cape with scalloped edges hung over one shoulder. White hair rimmed his bald head and swept upwards like a horned crest. His eyes blazed like fire. The stranger placed his hand over his mouth and swallowed.

My breath caught in my throat. "Did you just… eat Alice's ghost?" I stammered. "What are you?"

A corner of his thin-lipped mouth rose, and he stepped out of the wood grain, appearing as solid as any flesh and blood man. His pants flared out at the thighs and were tucked into black military boots. He pointed at the floor beneath my feet. A copper spider ringed its legs around the man's long index finger. I tried to step back from the spot, but the floor, carpet and all, lifted with my foot. I tried the other foot, but the floor adhered to my shoes like viscous goo. The more I pulled, the stickier the gelatinous tendrils became, as though I had stepped on a giant glue trap. There was no furniture to grab onto for stability.

The strange intruder closed his eyes and tilted his head back, but, like Alice, no sound left his mouth. My breathing remained the loudest thing in the room. An audible laugh wouldn't have been nearly so creepy as the silence.

"Can't you talk?" I shouted.

I twisted my waist and lunged, suddenly falling sideways and hitting solid floor. My fingers found comfort in perfectly normal carpet fibers.

Orange light accentuated the shadows in the room, flickering back and forth. The window blinds blazed. The man looked even more devilish framed by fire with his white hair swooping up like horns. Paint blistered and peeled as flames licked the ceiling, but the demon calmly smiled down at me, unfazed by the heat or the danger.

I shot up and made for the back door, but the devil now stood in the kitchen, blocking my path, calmly smiling as he had before. He wasn't even breathing hard.

Flames cascaded over the ceiling above my head. I turned back to the living room. The way was now clear. I glanced at the specter behind me as I ran for the door, but when I faced forward again, the demonic man stood in front of me once more. His head arched back again, and his chest shook with mute laughter.

"Is tormenting people fun for you?" I shouted. "We could both die in here!"

Blackness now stained the burning walls, and a flaming beam of wood fell in slow motion from the ceiling, barely missing me as I stepped out of the way. I imagined the cracks and pops one would expect in such an inferno, but the scene remained eerily quiet. It didn't seem possible that the fire could have spread so quickly! I hadn't smelled any chemical accelerant when I came in. Flames silhouetted my tormenter behind gray haze and waves of heat, but his glowing eyes pierced the smoke.

I covered my nose and mouth with my shirt, but then realized there was no smell of smoke. The demon stopped laughing for a moment.

All at once, pungent smoke filled my nose and stung my eyes. My lungs seized, and I coughed.

No matter which exit I tried, the demon would be there waiting for me. I only had one chance. I charged for the front door and the demonic man in my way. I might fail to push through him, but if I didn't try, I was sure to die in this house. The monster raised his hand in surprise and pointed the spider ring. I closed my eyes and smacked hard against the front door. Without looking back, I flung the door open and stumbled out into the dark, panting and coughing.

A cool breeze chilled my sweaty skin.

I turned my head to see the house intact. The front door opened into a dark living room, just as it had been when I arrived.

The demon was gone, as though it had all been some kind of waking nightmare. I let out one last cough, realizing there was no smoke or soot in my lungs.

The smoke hadn't felt real until I noticed it didn't smell, but then it became more intense than any smoke I'd ever experienced. I pulled the door shut and found my hand still shaking. Had it all been in my head? I backed away from the house and made my way across the street. Before unlocking my car, I looked back at the McGuiness house again as though I expected it to be different than before.

I was about to drive away when the cop pulled up. He was in one of the new Dodge Chargers the city had just purchased. A black nudge bar made the white bumper look like teeth as the car growled to a stop behind me.

I closed my eyes and breathed slowly. "I'm a professional," I said to myself. "Deep, regular breaths."

My face still glistened with sweat when I got out of the car and extended my hand, but he didn't take it.

"You the one that found her?" he asked.

My mind pulled back to Abby Duncan. "Yup. I'm afraid so." With all the strangeness, I'd almost forgotten about the poor woman.

"You her son or something?" the cop asked.

"No," I said. "I'm Jack Mahler, a PI working a case, and she called to give me some information."

The wind shifted, and I got a whiff of the cop's aftershave, the same cheap scent that hovered around Mrs. Duncan's body. It didn't necessarily mean anything. Thousands of men wore that scent.

I walked him around the house to the open back door. "When she didn't answer the door, I became suspicious. I saw her walker through the window and called to her, but she didn't answer."

"Was this door open when you arrived?" he asked.

"Yes."

He shot me a glance that told me he knew I was lying. The only way he could know that is if he'd been there earlier that night.

I scanned the name on his uniform. "Officer S. Decker," I said.

"Yeah."

"I recognize your name from the accident report for Mrs. McGuiness from across the street. You were the first officer on the scene."

Decker made his way inside and looked down at the dead woman. "Yeah. So?"

"I'm doing a routine investigation for her life insurance policy."

His face jerked up. "I didn't know she had a life insurance policy."

"Is there any reason you would know that?"

"Nope." He looked back to Abigail on the floor. "Well, looks like she's dead. Coroner's on his way." He glared at me. "I'll see you around, Jack."

The way he said it chilled me to the marrow. "Sure. See you around."

I sat in my car and stared at the peaceful suburban street in front of me. If Officer Decker had killed Abby Duncan, the only possible reason was that Stevie had seen her talking to me. This was supposed to be an easy case. Now there were scientific secrets, a ghost, and a rogue cop! The phantasm in that burning house didn't scare me half as much as Officer Decker.

Why can't anything be simple?

CHAPTER 4

Maybe my subconscious could make more sense of all this after a good night's sleep. My building reminded me of a 1950's motel, with outdoor entrances to the rooms and an open air pool in the center of the L-shaped building. I walked through the gap in the stucco wall by the pool and noticed light pouring out the open door to my second story studio apartment. The entrance to my room lay right at the top of the half-turn, metal framed stairs. I pulled my gun and crept up the cement steps.

Diane had her back to the door as she bent over the bed taking the leash off Alpha. Her black dress hugged round hips, showing off curves I didn't know she had. Shoulder and back muscles rippled visibly under smooth, dark brown skin within the backless dress. The dress ended just above the knees when she stood. This wasn't a dog walking outfit. The sneakers on her feet didn't match the dress but seemed more her style. Tight black curls dusted her round head.

I hated leashes, but Diane insisted on using them, and the dogs didn't seem to mind as long as somebody walked them. Alpha was a little dog, about twelve pounds. He certainly had some terrier in him. Tufts of fur on his brows exaggerated and humanized his expressions. Gray peppered the dark fur around his nose and resembled an old man's mustache. His pointed ears rose toward me, waiting for me to respond.

Meega remained lying on the floor, but thumped her tail when she saw me. Meega weighed about thirty pounds. White and black speckled her short, red fur.

Thankfully, I managed to return the gun to its holster before Diane turned around. That could have been embarrassing.

"Oh," she said. "I didn't expect you back yet. They're all walked. I was about to give them their treats."

I continued to stare.

"What?" she asked.

"You…"

She smiled and did a little pirouette. "Yes…?"

I stepped inside, away from the breeze, and quickly grabbed my nose. "You're wearing way too much perfume."

Her smile twisted. "Women wear perfume on dates, Jack. I'm starting the weekend early! Did you think I was spending my whole evening with your dogs? I get two free weekends a month, and I'm not spending them running your errands!" Diane's ex had their son, Reece, every other weekend. Reece was an awesome kid. He loved the dogs, and they loved him.

"No," I said. "Of course not. I just don't like perfume. You know I'm sensitive to that stuff."

She gave a tight-lipped smile and grabbed her purse. "Well, fortunately for me, I am not going on a date with *you* tonight!"

She made it halfway down the steps before I could respond. "Wait," I called. "Diane, you look… nice— really nice."

Without turning around, she extended her middle finger back at me. "Stay out of trouble, Jack. I'll see you Monday."

I started to close the door, but Alpha and Meega both cocked their heads at me. "What?" I pushed the door open again and called down to Diane, "Have fun! Don't do anything I wouldn't do!"

She smiled. "You mean like go on a date with an actual human being?"

"Ouch! Very funny, Diane!" I knew she was just teasing, but that stung a little. I had too much baggage to date anyone seriously right now. Maybe after I saved a little more money up, got a new car and a bigger place to live, I'd finally feel like meeting people again.

I scratched the dogs behind their ears and gave them each a treat before releasing my hair from the tiny rubber band that held it back. I ran my fingers through the tangles on the back of my head.

Alpha circled around, looked up at me and waited. I was a soft touch, and gave both dogs another treat.

* * *

Soft track lighting lit the long, rectangular room, but a brown haze hung over everything except the pale blue coffin at the far end. Shadowy figures sat in rows of chairs. I followed a path down the center aisle. A dog barked somewhere in the distance.

I looked peaceful and relaxed, lying in the coffin. Pink scalp showed through the brown hair on top of my head. It had thinned much more than I had realized. My eyebrows had been shaved and shaped so my unibrow didn't show, and my hair was tied back into a pony tail— classy. The mortician had done a good job on me.

The barking came closer, still muffled, but louder. The walls thumped three times.

Something brushed my bare leg, and I realized I wasn't wearing any pants. I covered my crotch with my hands and looked over my shoulder at the shadowy audience. If I didn't turn around, maybe they wouldn't notice. It seemed logical at the time. I slid around the back of the coffin where my legs were hidden.

Most of the audience remained shadowy and indistinct, but I recognized Diane in the front row with Reece. She cried and held Luis' hand. Luis was short but broad-shouldered. With his lingering looks and borderline inappropriate compliments, I had often suspected he had more than just a professional interest in Diane. Heightened emotions made my funeral the perfect moment for him to make a play.

Allen, the policeman, sat on the other side of the room next to my mom. But Mom had passed away three years ago. She died never knowing if I was alive or dead.

If Mom could be here, I wondered if Dad was here somewhere as well. I scanned the shadowy rows. Would I even recognize him if he was here? He hadn't been around when I was growing up; why should it be any different now that I'm dead? It wasn't his fault he'd gotten killed in the Gulf War. I'd grown up hearing what a hero he had been, but when I tried to follow in his footsteps, I failed so spectacularly. I not only disgraced myself, I dishonored my family and my dad's memory.

Dogs continued barking just outside the room. Didn't they realize what a solemn occasion this was? I looked back to the coffin and found the other me staring back. Instead of eyes, tiny moons glowed in his sockets. He bared shark-like teeth and snapped his jaws at me.

I fell away, and the back of my head landed on a soft pillow. Blue light from the window accentuated a slim, angular body floating above my bed like a weightless phantom. The demon hovered with folded arms and studied me in the dark with glowing eyes. My lungs refused to breath. I tried to move, but only my finger twitched. My heart pounded in my chest, and I sank as deep into the mattress as I could. All four of Meega's legs were planted firmly on the bed, though the bum one quaked. The hair on her back stood up, and she bared her teeth at the apparition. Alpha hopped on and off the bed, yipping nervously.

Mr. Gibson next door thumped three times on our shared wall. He hated dogs, and I wasn't supposed to have pets in the apartment. The noise shocked me back to my senses.

I sucked in a breath of air and grabbed my gun from the holster next to the bed. When I looked up again, my tormenter was gone. My gun pointed at the door across from the foot of the bed.

The neighbor thumped the wall again. I scooped up Alpha, interrupting him mid-yip, and flipped on the light. He was shaking, still staring where the phantom had floated. Meega's back spasmed when I stroked her, and she looked back at me with concern.

"It's okay," I said. "It's gone."

I couldn't *see* the apparition anymore, but was it really gone? The monster tormenting Alice McGuiness had followed me home! It could still be lurking invisibly right above the bed where it had been. If not for the dogs waking me, I would have thought the coffin had just been a nightmare, but I wondered how much of the dream was from my own subconscious and how much was the malevolent influence of this bogeyman.

Dreams about your own death are said to be omens of real life tragedy. People even say Abraham Lincoln dreamed about his own death before his assassination. Fortunately, I didn't have any theatre plans in my near future.

I helped Meega off the bed so she wouldn't further hurt her bad leg. I had lived in this apartment six months before finally buying this bed. Before that, the dogs and I all slept on the floor, huddled in the corner with blankets. The first time Diane offered to check on the dogs, I realized how weird that might look and decided I needed to buy a bed.

The dogs and I were much too agitated to go straight back to sleep. I threw on some clothes and opened the door, but I didn't bother with leashes. I noted the spot on the door where my bullet would have hit after passing through the phantasm, then looked at the bed, and thought of the bullet in Stevie's wall.

Must have been some nightmare.

This was beyond my ability to deal with.

I needed someone who could talk to the dead.

CHAPTER 5

Every case of unnatural death in New Mexico ends up in the Office of the Medical Investigator at the New Mexico Scientific Laboratories building. They buzzed me in and directed me downstairs. Security was almost as intense as at Sandia, but at least here they let me keep my phone.

Stevie and Alice had signed all the necessary releases when they took out the insurance policy. The Medical Examiner, Dr. Kakali Bhatia, sipped her coffee and looked over my paperwork. She kept the thick dark hair circling her soft round face short, possibly to keep it from dangling into dead people's guts, but I didn't want to think about that. Dark lipstick stained the edge of her coffee mug. I didn't know how she could drink coffee surrounded by all that bleach and decay.

"Okay," she said. "I can get you a copy of my report and the death certificate."

"I've already got that," I said.

"Then what do you need from me?" she asked.

"I'm looking for what wasn't in the report."

"I'm very thorough."

"But you didn't do a full autopsy?"

"The cause of death was no mystery. The airbag didn't deploy. Poor girl's face was smashed to pieces in the accident. She hit that tree at around thirty-five miles per hour, which may not sound so fast, but thirty-five miles per hour can shatter hard bones and split organs. I thought for sure it would be a closed casket funeral, but the mortician managed to put her face back together. Harper's does great work."

"I'll keep that in mind if I ever need a mortician." I remembered my dream the night before and seeing myself dead in a coffin.

Dr. Bhatia took a sip of coffee and smiled. "We all need a mortician sooner or later."

"I suppose." I wondered how she could be so cheerful. Seeing death every day must have made her numb. "Did you do a tox screen on her?" I asked.

"That's standard. It all came back negative. No drugs or alcohol in her system."

"Would prescription sleep aids show up on the screen?"

"It depends. Which sleep aids?"

I stumbled over the pronunciation…"Flunitrazepam and galantamine."

Dr. Bhatia scrunched her nose.

"What?" I asked.

"Flunitrazepam is a benzodiazepine and would be detected, but… Are you sure you have the names right?"

"I made sure to write them down exactly as written on the bottles. Why?"

"Flunitrazepam isn't legal in the United States. It's a fantastic sleep aid, but can produce temporary amnesia and was implicated in several cases of drug-induced sexual assault."

"A date rape drug?"

"That's what the media calls it, yes, but it really is one of the best sleep aids out there. Galantamine, I believe, is used to treat Alzheimer's. The patient was 33, a little young for that, even with early onset."

"A drug to make you forget and a drug to make you remember? They both had *for the treatment of sleeplessness* written on the bottles."

"You must have gotten the names wrong."

"Thanks for your help."

Once back in the wagon, I retrieved my laptop and looked up flunitrazepam and galantamine. I checked my photo of the pill bottles to confirm my spelling.

Side effects of flunitrazepam, besides short-term memory loss, include loss of inhibition, visual disturbances, vivid dreams, confusion, loss of musculoskeletal control, slurred speech, decreased blood pressure, gastrointestinal disturbances, urinary retention, blah blah.

Galantamine actually can be used to promote sleep, but it isn't common. It can also cause nausea, digestion issues, sleep paralysis, increased dream retention, depression, dehydration, etc. It's available over the counter as an unregulated supplement as well as by prescription to treat memory problems.

Flunitrazepam wasn't even legal in the United States, so how did the doctor prescribe it and a pharmacist fill it? I remembered old Abby mentioning Alice's slurred speech, but the M.E. didn't find any drugs or alcohol in Alice's system.

Only one person could tell me for certain why and how these drugs were prescribed.

CHAPTER 6

The generic office building blended in with others around it. I took the elevator to the fifth floor and found my way to a wood and glass door marked *Doctor David Brown PhD.*

The blond wood of the walls and front desk matched the arms and legs of the cushy waiting room chairs. It wasn't a large waiting room— only enough chairs for six people if they were packed in. Magazines sat on the tables and a small play area with kid's books and colorful building blocks lay in one corner.

"Do you have an appointment?" The receptionist asked. She was a hefty woman with wavy black hair and a headset phone over her ear.

"No," I said. "I'm working for Net Life. I'm here to ask Dr. Brown about a former patient."

"Patient information is confidential."

I presented my release forms.

She glanced at them and studied me skeptically. "He's with a patient now and has another appointment in fifteen minutes."

"I'll wait. I don't need to talk to him very long. Maybe he can fit me in."

I sat back and tried to relax. Only one other person sat in the waiting area, a slender man with thinning hair and glasses. A Sandia Research ID badge hung off his belt.

On a muted flat screen television in the corner I caught the tail end of one of Luis' commercials. An agent pointed a giant camera out a car window. Cut to a couple embracing within a curtained window. The closed caption didn't pick up the dialogue, but I knew what it said. "Cheating spouse? Missing person?" A man used crutches to reach his mailbox, then tossed them aside and jumped up and down upon receiving a check in the mail. "When you need to know the truth and you need it now..." Luis folded his arms over his broad chest and looked into the camera, trying to look tough. You probably wouldn't find him that intimidating in person. Luis stood half a head shorter than me, but his wide shoulders looked good on television with no one standing next to him. As cheesy as I found them, the commercials worked. When you needed a PI in New Mexico, Navarro Investigations was likely the first name you thought of.

A door opened and a woman with bright red hair emerged. Her pink scrubs stank of cigarettes, and she dabbed her running mascara with a tissue, evidently composing herself after an emotional moment with the doctor. Dr. Brown waddled out behind her. The receptionist whispered in the doctor's ear. I caught a glimpse of him, and my heart froze.

I didn't believe my eyes. He was pudgier than I remembered. A film of grease covered his pale skin. A crest of thin, white hair rimmed his bald head. When he looked up, I knew I was not mistaken. I sprang to my feet, trigger finger itching to pull my gun. "Dr. Bohman!"

The doctor pursed his lips and his eyes grew wide with confusion and surprise. "Do I know you?"

I almost laughed. Dr. Bohman had done my intake evaluation for Catalyst, a survivalist militia which dabbled in mysticism and fringe science. It had taken me eleven years to climb out of the pit they'd left me in. I never looked for them, never even did a Google search because I was so scared they would somehow know and track me down. But my life was so insignificant to them that Dr. Bohman didn't even recognize me!

I marched forward, nostrils flaring as I tried to contain my anger. "You really don't remember?" I growled.

The receptionist dialed three digits on the phone.

Dr. Bohman slowly raised his hands and spoke in a calm monotone. "Whoever you think I am, you must be mistaken." Even though he moved slowly, I flinched when he gently placed his left hand on my shoulder. "My name is Dr. David Brown." He moved his right hand forward, and I caught the flash of a copper ring. Electricity arced between the mandibles of a metal spider and shot from my neck into the carpet beneath me. My body jerked, and the floor hit my back.

Bruises on top of bruises.

Kind gray eyes looked down at me. I'd recognize those cheekbones anywhere, even without the blue uniform. "Allen," I said in awe. Ever since he had saved my life and the life of my dog, I'd had a weird fixation on Officer Allen Deschene. His face was stern, but I knew the kindness he was capable of.

I sat up too fast and my temple flared with new pain. The redhead was gone, but another woman, Bohman's next appointment, had joined the man who had been waiting. They exchanged glances with one another as they watched me.

"Where's the doctor?" I asked.

"Gone," Allen said. "They say Dr. Brown ran off after he knocked you out."

"His name isn't Dr. Brown," I said. "He had some sort of stun gun in his ring."

"In his ring?" Allen said.

I held a chair for support and stiffly pulled myself into a standing position. "In his ring," I repeated." My muscles ached like I'd just run a marathon.

Allen raised his eyebrows and shook his head. "Only you, Mahler."

"I knew him by the name Dr. Bohman eleven years ago, but that could just be another alias for all I know. He must have freaked out when I recognized him."

The receptionist's brow furrowed. Her eyes grew wide when I focused on her.

"How long have you worked for the doctor?" I asked.

She stammered. "About two years. Right after he opened this practice. I found the job opening on Career Builder. He needed someone to handle billing and scheduling."

I shuddered. All this time Dr. Bohman had an office five minutes from my apartment. "You from around here?" I asked.

"Yes," she squeaked.

"You have family here who can confirm that?"

Allen pulled me back and whispered, "I'll check her out. You need to calm down."

He was right. I clenched my hand into a fist to keep it from shaking and sank into a waiting room chair. The patients subtly inched away from me in their seats.

"You can leave," Allen said to the patients. "We'll contact you if we have more questions."

"Wait," I said. "What kind of questions did the doctor ask you in there?" I motioned my head toward the treatment room.

The female patient became angry. "I have to get back to work."

"Back to Sandia?" I said.

Her eyes widened.

I looked to the man. "You work there too, don't you?"

The man hesitated, but answered, "Yes."

Allen interceded. "I have your contact info. Someone will contact you later if we need anything more."

The woman left immediately. The man nodded as he stood and thanked Allen on his way out, casting a suspicious glance at me as he left.

"What was that all about?" Allen asked.

"This is big," I said. "Very big. All Dr. Bohman's patients had connections to top secret energy projects. I think he was stealing research."

I walked behind the reception desk. "We need to look through his records!"

The receptionist blocked my path and looked to Allen for support.

The policeman grabbed my arm. "You know you can't do that."

My face flushed, and I felt like an amateur. "Can you get a warrant?"

"This is above my pay grade. We'll put a guard on his office. If what you say pans out, the FBI will subpoena his records."

I slumped in a chair and nodded. "Allen?" I said.

"Yes?"

"How well do you know Officer Decker?"

"Stan Decker? From night shift?"

I nodded. "Do you trust him?"

Allen hesitated. "A cop has to trust all his fellow officers. It's a matter of survival."

"But do you *really* trust him?" I asked.

The corner of Allen's mouth tightened and he shrugged a shoulder. "He takes the lazy way out sometimes, but yeah, I trust him to get the job done. Why?"

I wanted to tell Allen everything, but I'd already dropped so many bombs that afternoon, and I had no actual proof Decker was involved.

The door to the treatment room hung open. I stood, and Allen followed me in. A vinyl couch matched a big chair, and a box of tissues sat under a lamp on the table. Next to the tissues was…

"He's made improvements." I picked up what looked like a tinker toy made into a geodesic dome. I pointed out the electrodes on the interior. "If you were to wear this on your head, the electrodes would touch your skull and measure your brainwaves at specific points. Bohman made all the Catalyst recruits wear electrodes on our heads when he interviewed us. There was no rigid structure like this back then. Each electrode had to be placed individually on our heads."

Allen picked it up and turned it over. "Why would he do that?"

I shrugged. "He said he could tell if we were lying. I thought it sounded pretty dumb, but I was desperate for a job at the time, any job, and I figured there was no harm in it. I assumed it was just a trick— we would be afraid to lie for fear it might actually work. But maybe it really did give him a glimpse inside our heads. "

"There's no power source or cords," Allen said. "You sure it's not just a fancy toy?"

The thought of putting it on my own head to demonstrate made me queasy. I certainly wasn't going to put it on Allen. The receptionist was cancelling appointments by phone at her desk with silent tears in her eyes. I showed her the helmet. "You ever see Bohman use this?"

She hung up and shook her head.

"Put it on," I said.

She hesitated, but I placed it over her wavy hair before she could resist. Nothing happened. I adjusted the fit and tiny LED lights, unnoticed before, came to life. Something hummed back in the office, and the receptionist's entire body relaxed. Lines in her forehead that I hadn't notice before eased away, and her eyes glazed over. Allen supported her to make sure she didn't fall out of her chair.

Back in the treatment room, I found a computer monitor hidden under the glass surface of the desk. Three lines oscillated up and down, changing colors when they crossed each other.

"Mahler!" Allen called. "This isn't safe."

The oscilloscope suddenly went dead, and I found Allen had removed the helmet.

The receptionist blinked as though she were waking from a nap. "Did I fall asleep?" she said. "I think I was dreaming. Do I still have a job?"

Allen and I traded a look of concern. "No," I said. "I don't think you do." I checked my phone and saw I was going to be late picking Larry up from the bus stop. There was nothing left for me to do here. I turned to Allen. "Call me when you have more info."

Allen nodded and remained behind with the receptionist. I found my way back to the parking garage and wished I'd parked a little closer. I hadn't planned on being knocked out and bruised up again. At least I could bill Net Life for the parking fee. I'd have a harder time finding a way to bill for Larry's services. I'd most likely be out his bus fare here, but I needed help on this, and he was the only person I could think of to call.

Before I started the car, I took the laptop from the trunk and fired it up. My hands shook as I typed. It was strange that I had never done this before now. With a deep breath, I typed *Catalyst* into the browser.

Catalyst—substance that provokes or accelerates a chemical change without itself being changed; a person or thing that precipitates change.

A standard definition. I found no mention of scary militias or twisted science clubs. Perhaps Catalyst didn't exist anymore. Maybe Dr. Bohman was working solo as a free agent. Or maybe Catalyst had managed to keep a low profile while I'd been away.

Catalyst claimed society was in decline. Like their namesake, they wanted to accelerate the fall of civilization and believed they could create a new, better world from the ashes of the old. They collected people who, through brains or strength, would be the foundation of this new world. Besides strength, they also liked people easy to manipulate. I had been a tool to them— raw material, no different than I had been to the military.

I snapped the laptop shut and started the car.

Before I backed the car up, I opened the laptop again and found Dr. Brown's website. There was no picture of him, just a list of his qualifications... *PhD, University of Georgia, 1994; MA Psychology, Catholic University, 1985; BA Sociology, Temple University, 1980...* and a list of conditions he treated. He had five stars on Yelp. Seriously, mad Dr. Bohman had five stars!

"Accepting new patients by referral only," I read out loud. "Only patients who work at Sandia Labs, I bet."

CHAPTER 7

Traffic downtown was busy, but not as bad as it could have been on a Friday afternoon. The wagon squeaked to a stop. Some teens loitered in the red brick plaza outside the Greyhound Station. I wondered why they weren't in school, but that wasn't any of my business. A petite man with brown mop-top hair and round glasses hopped in my car and tossed a small canvas bag in the back. Larry's hair and glasses kind of reminded me of John Denver. He wore a white tunic shirt with gold trim and reeked of patchouli oil, what I called *hippy smell*. I'd met Lawrence (Larry) Papakis on a case a while ago. I didn't know him well, but he came highly recommended.

"Hey Jack," he said. "You're late."

"I was unexpectedly detained," I said. "Thanks for coming so quickly."

"I knew you wouldn't have called unless it was really important."

I bought Larry lunch before heading over to Rio Rancho. I was craving a Blakes's Lotta Burger, but Larry was a vegetarian. We finally settled on a sit down Mexican place, and he got vegetarian fajitas. It took only a little longer than fast food. The price wasn't much more either, and the food was delicious. They made the salsa fresh at the restaurant and the steak in my burrito had that wonderful charred flavor.

"I'm actually glad you called me up here," Larry said. "I need some help."

"You need a PI?"

"No, nothing like that. There are a few Indian reservations around Albuquerque. I thought maybe you could point me to a shaman familiar with Native American folklore regarding shape shifters."

I flexed one of my hands and my knuckles popped. "What would I know about shape shifters?"

Larry smiled like he knew something he shouldn't. "I thought since you live up here, you might have some contacts with the local tribes."

I narrowed my eyes at the vegetarian. "There was animal lard in those refried beans you just ate."

Larry lifted his eyebrows. "What is this sudden negativity about?"

I got up to pay the check, suddenly angry and not quite sure why. Larry claimed to talk to spirits. A day ago, I wouldn't have believed it, but today I wondered what those spirits had been telling him. I had invited him here to help with Alice, not to nose around in my business.

Larry followed me out to the car. "Did I say something to upset you?"

Larry was in to all sorts of weird stuff. I realized not everything was about me. "Forget about it. It's been a strange couple of days and I'm probably more irritable than normal, but that's no excuse for me to be an ass. I really am grateful to have you here. I'm at an impasse on this case. I don't know anything about ghosts or spirits. I need the help of an expert."

"I doubt any living person can be called an expert on the afterlife, but I've got more experience than most."

Despite making amends, it was still a quiet drive. Larry let his arm hang out the open window and watched the world fly by. I clicked on the radio and invited him to pick a station.

Larry wheeled through static and settled on a soft eighties synthesizer. "Lady in Red" came out of the functional speaker in tinny mono. The wind and the road faded into the background as Chris de Burgh's haunting vocal played. I thought of poor Alice in her red dress and wondered if a person could still feel pain after they died.

We finally pulled up to Stevie's house in Rio Rancho. The door to the house remained unlocked from the night before. I half expected to smell smoke, but the house was exactly as I had left it, empty of furniture and debris.

Larry dropped his satchel in the corner and circled the room. Returning to his bag, he pulled out a one and a half foot gold rod. Green ribbons drifted around the wand as he waved it around the room. "Spirits of the house, by the power of the Caduceus, I command you to appear."

I normally didn't buy into this talking to spirits thing, but Larry was well respected by a very cynical acquaintance of mine. Still, watching him circle the room waving those ribbons and shouting into empty space looked pretty silly. He looked more like a baton twirler than some kind of exorcist.

Larry climbed the stairs with the wand held in front of him. I followed in the wake of his patchouli cloud. He waved the wand from side to side and then made his way to the bedroom. "The Caducifer commands! Spirits awaken! Alice McGuiness, come forth!"

Larry seemed to be zeroing in on the bullet hole in the wall, but turned to me and shrugged. "No ghosts here."

"There has to be!"

He held up the wand. "I've got the Caduceus. If there were spirits here, they would be forced to manifest."

I gazed through the window at old Abby's house across the street. "Is it possible this bogeyman is a real life demon who took Alice's ghost away?"

Larry's eyes softened. "Then there should still be some trace of the entity. We would at least be able to discover which hell she was taken to, but there is nothing here."

I turned to Larry. "There's more than one hell?"

He nodded.

"And I thought just being dead was bad."

"I'm afraid there are much worse things than death."

"Poor Alice. She just wanted what all of us want, someone to love her."

"It isn't common for demons to physically manifest on earth like this," Larry said. "Not unless someone here summoned it."

My mind drifted to husband Stevie. He had to be in on the plot but didn't seem the type to put on dark robes and chant or whatever one did to summon evil spirits. Either did mad scientist Dr. Bohman for that matter. What did rogue scientists, stolen energy plans and dirty cops have to do with summoning literal demons? "What about rings?" I asked.

"What about them?"

"Could a ring be used to summon a …whatever this is?"

"Special rings can be sacred to specific entities, and rings are sometimes used to bind djin."

"Djin—genies—like Barbara Eden?"

"Something like that. Demons, angels, djin, faeries; not all spirits are ghosts of people."

"*Faeries,* that's a real thing?"

"Different cultures look at the same beings in different ways."

I raised my eyebrows and shook my head, suddenly feeling very small in a big, mysterious world. "So our bogeyman could be like the king of the fairy people or something?"

I was half joking and hoped Larry might give me a little chuckle to ease my anxiety, but instead he shrugged. "Maybe. There are lots of old stories about faeries causing mischief and abducting humans."

I shook my head and sighed. "What about a ring with a stun gun in it?"

Larry let his mouth hang open for a moment, then scrunched one eye.

I explained, "Dr. Bohman and the demon had the same ring design."

"It can't be a coincidence, but a *stun gun*? Are you sure?"

"I've got the bruises to prove it. Not the first time I've been tazed."

A crooked smile bloomed across Larry's face. "I don't doubt that."

We had nothing more to gain there. After a few cranks, I got the wagon started and we swung by the cemetery. A mound of fresh earth covered Alice's grave, with only a single, red rose. I lifted the flower and sniffed the air around it. Stevie had been here, but no ghosts appeared for us today. If Stevie had helped kill her, why leave a fresh flower on her grave?

I pulled the car over a few miles down the road. Broad gouges marred the tree where Alice's car had hit it. The tree would heal, but the scars in the bark would linger, a memorial to Alice as long as the tree remained alive. I walked away from the scars, staring at the pavement as I did. Twenty-four feet from the tree, despite what the accident report had said, I did indeed find skid marks, but they weren't brake marks. Brake marks start light and become darker. These started dark and became lighter. The car had *accelerated* into the tree!

I got out my camera and took pictures of the tree and the skid marks. A car eased by, and I moved aside. The police cruiser crawled past, and Officer Decker glowered at me from the driver's seat. It left me cold.

With photos of these skid marks, my job was technically over. The insurance company could deny the claim, saying this was a suicide. Luis would probably give me a big bonus for saving the insurance company 500,000 bucks. But there was too much going on here that I couldn't ignore. A little more time wouldn't hurt. Decker had murdered someone in order to keep a secret, and he knew that I knew. But I had no proof, and he was a cop. It wasn't good to have a cop as an enemy.

CHAPTER 8

I had no luck contacting Doc Ellison by phone. He didn't seem the type to take a Friday off, but security at the lab said he wasn't in. I dropped Larry off at Bien Mur Indian Market on the way to Ellison's house. It would be a pain to drive back for Larry later, but it would keep him out of my hair, and even if he didn't find what he was looking for, I hoped he would enjoy browsing the Indian crafts. Tourists seemed to like it. If he got bored, he could always play slots at the casino next door.

It was well into the afternoon, but Ellison came to the door wearing men's pajamas, the kind I'd only seen on television.

"Not feeling well?" I asked.

Ellison turned and I followed him inside. "You know I never hugged her?" Evidently, Doc felt chatty.

"Never?"

"Not since she was 9 years old. If I could just go back and give her one hug. That time is gone now. It's no wonder she hates me."

"Do you really think she hated you?"

"Why else would she…"

"What?" I asked.

"You will think I am insane."

"You'd be surprised at the crazy things I've heard and seen."

"She visited me last night."

Hope washed over me. I thought the demon might have really eaten Alice, or drug her to some unimaginable hell forever.

"Was that the first time you saw Alice's ghost?"

"You don't seem surprised."

"I've seen her too. So did Stevie."

"*Stevie*," he repeated. "He was really spying on me?"

The FBI must have started asking questions at Sandia labs. News travels fast.

"I think so," I said. "His contact was Dr. Brown... I knew him as Dr. Bohman."

Ellison shook his head. "But Stephen was such a nice boy, so good for my..." His words trailed off and he covered his face with one hand.

"I'm sorry," I said.

"I trusted him with my little girl."

"Last night was the first night you saw her ghost?"

He nodded. "Yes."

"She didn't appear to you until Stevie disappeared. She couldn't find Stevie, so she reached out to you."

He looked at me, taking in the details.

"How did she look?" I asked. "What did she do?"

He motioned to the kitchen door. "I came home from work so late. I was exhausted, and thought I dreamt her, but I didn't wake up. I walked around her, waved my arms, testing for some sort of light projector."

"Did you find any?" I asked. I was surprised by Dr. Ellison's cold cynicism in the face of such a personal apparition, but I was also impressed. *I* had never thought to walk around her and look for a trick.

Ellison shook his head. "She scowled at me. I was so frightened. She seemed to be reprimanding me for being so cold, even to her ghost. I tried to talk to her, but she wouldn't answer. I apologized for everything I'd done, or rather, hadn't done." Quiet tears fell from Ellison's eyes.

"Then what happened?"

"She turned away and just sort of…" he waved his hands in the air, searching for the words. "She kind of collapsed into a sparkling mist and was gone."

"Was there anyone else there?"

He looked confused. "I live alone."

"No other ghosts or… apparitions or anything?"

"Who else would there be?"

I tried to smile. I didn't want to worry him. "I don't know." It wasn't a total lie. I knew there was another apparition, but, though I called it a demon, I didn't know who or what it was.

"If I had it to do all over again…" he said. "You only get one chance to show people how important they are. I've never been good with people. Even my own daughter was a stranger."

I put a hand on his shoulder. "Who knows," I said. "If ghosts are real, then maybe there are second chances."

A switch seemed to go off in Ellison's head. Instant calm washed over him. "Maybe. Yes… Perhaps."

CHAPTER 9

We watched people walking in and out of the post office.
Larry's bare feet hung out the passenger window.

"Do you have to do that?" I asked.

"What?" he asked.

"Leave your feet dangling out like that. We are supposed to
be inconspicuous."

"But it's hot out, and everyone's got feet." He wiggled his
toes for emphasis.

I shook my head and changed the subject. "Did you find
what you were looking for at the market?"

Larry shrugged a shoulder. "Not exactly. Some people tried
to sell me some trinkets— dream catchers and things. I don't think
they took me seriously. I did get some phone numbers though."

While Larry was talking, my phone vibrated. It was a text
from Luis asking if my report was done yet. I didn't know what to
say back. This was supposed to be a simple report. I had expected
to be done yesterday. I began to type that this was going to take a
little longer, but heard a click behind me.

I stiffened. In the side mirror I saw Stevie's right arm. I
noticed the symbol on his ring, an arrow with a triangle above it.
I later learned this was a chemistry symbol for a catalyst. He held
a gun under a folded newspaper and pointed it right at my head.
He'd come up downwind.

"I'm impressed," I said, still staring forward. "I'm a hard
guy to sneak up on."

"How'd you know I'd be here?" Stevie asked.

"Figured you'd be checking your P.O. box. Wouldn't want to miss any insurance checks."

Larry brought his feet into the car. He must have finally seen the gun. "What the hell?"

"Stay calm, Larry," I said. "He won't kill us out in the open like this. That's not his style. He's the type to kill old ladies in their kitchen and make it look like natural causes."

"Jack!" Larry whispered. "Don't antagonize him!"

Stevie's voice quaked. "I wasn't the one who did that! She should have kept her nose out of my business. So should you!"

"If you didn't want people in your business," I said. "You shouldn't have filed that insurance claim."

Stevie remained quiet. He was distracted enough that I might be able to duck out of the path of his gun and get away, but at this range and with my movement restricted in the car, it was far from a sure thing. Even if I managed to get away, the bullet meant for me might hit Larry, or a pedestrian. My only option was to keep him talking and hope an advantage would present itself.

"They didn't know," I said. "Did they? Your masters—Catalyst. They didn't know you opened a policy on your wife. You're in big trouble."

"Jack!" Larry said

"Tell me, Stevie," I continued, "How much of that dating profile was yours and how much was created by Dr.... Brown is it today?"

Stevie lowered the gun. "None of it was me. It was all Dr. Bohman, tailored to Alice's profile."

With his gun lowered, I felt emboldened and turned my head to face him. "Did you even write your own messages to her?"

"Of course," he said. "Under Dr. Bohman's supervision. I needed practice before I met her in person."

I shook my head. "You must be some actor, but no one can maintain a role 24/7. Must have been torture living with a woman you had nothing in common with all those months. No wonder you fought. No wonder you killed her."

"I didn't!"

"Somebody did. A friend of yours, I bet. Decker maybe? What I can't figure out is why. You got in with Alice, and that got you close to her father so you could steal his secrets, but why kill her? Did she learn too much about the real you?"

"It started after our first counseling session with Dr. Bohman. He was supposed to be my handler, my liaison to Catalyst. He gave me my orders and I fed him information, but after he talked to Alice, he lost all interest in me. For a while, there was another patient he was focused on too, but soon it was all about Alice."

"What was his interest in Alice?"

"I don't know."

"And why kill her?"

"I don't know."

"But you had to know she was in danger. Why else take out the insurance policy?"

"Dr. Bohman had an interest in her. Things don't go well for people Bohman is interested in."

An involuntary shiver ran up my body. I hoped no one noticed.

Larry finally spoke again, "No wonder she haunts you."

Stevie bent down to eye my passenger, and Larry did not look away. "Yes," Stevie said. "She haunts me. She was a good woman. She was! She deserved better. It was too easy, really. She had already isolated herself. We cut her off from friends and family. I was the only person she trusted, and I was a fraud."

At that moment, I thought I understood why we didn't see the ghost at the house that morning. "She doesn't haunt the house. She haunts you!"

Tears pooled in Stevie's eyes. "No. She doesn't come to me anymore. Not since I left the house. She tortured me every night since it happened, scared the shit out of me, but now that she's gone... really gone... I miss her so much."

"What about the demon?" I asked. "Do you miss him?"

Stevie's reddened eyes shot up. "You've seen him too?"

"Skinny guy, green cape, white hair?"

Stevie nodded.

"I saw him pluck Alice's ghost out of the air and swallow her."

Larry spoke from the passenger seat. "Somehow Alice got herself trapped between worlds."

"Oh," Stevie trilled. He spun around and sat on the curb with his head between his knees. "Like her life wasn't bad enough. She's got to be tortured when she's dead too, and it's my fault."

Slowly, so not to startle Stevie, I got out of the car and sat beside him. The gun rested at his side, but I wasn't worried about it anymore. "What is that B-movie reject?"

Stevie shrugged. "He started showing up after Alice…" His voice trailed off.

"You never saw him before that?" I asked. "What about Alice? Did she ever see him?"

"I think she would have mentioned something like that."

"This demon has to have some connection to Bohman."

"Maybe. Probably."

"Stevie, if you really want to help Alice, then Larry here is your new best friend."

CHAPTER 10

"Jack," Larry whispered. "Are you sure this is a good idea?"

I looked in the rearview mirror and saw Stevie hunched in the back seat like a defeated, broken man. "He won't hurt us," I said. I'd frisked him and taken his gun. I may be trusting, but I'm not that stupid.

The setting sun cast long shadows between houses and bathed the Sandia Mountains in ruby-red light. A large bird, an eagle or hawk, perched on top of Abigail Duncan's house. I couldn't determine its color in the fading light. It lowered its head, watching us. In old stories, birds are said to foretell the coming of death. They eat corpses and show up when it's about to be feeding time. I hoped we weren't on the menu.

I tore my eyes away from the bird and flipped on the lights in the McGuiness living room. If anyone harassed us about being here, we had the legal homeowner with us. Stevie meandered around the empty room as if reliving old memories.

"Where did she most often appear to you?" Larry asked.

Stevie gazed up the darkened stairs. "The bedroom."

Larry nodded. "Then maybe we will have better luck there." Larry waited at the foot of the steps.

Stevie looked to Larry, then at me, before finally ascending the stairs. We followed close behind. Stevie's breathing became irregular, and I could smell his sweat as he reached for the light switch in his former bedroom. The switch clicked, but no lights came on.

"You couldn't even leave a lamp, could you?" I said.

Stevie turned to me but didn't seem to know what to say. "Maybe this was a bad idea."

"No," Larry said, brandishing his gold wand. "There is someone here. Show yourself!"

A shadow passed in front of the window.

Larry continued, "By the power of the—"

"Larry," I whispered.

We all turned to the window. Alice's dress merged with the dim, red light outside. Dark circles fell like shadows below her eyes. Her cheeks had pulled inward as though she were wasting away. Alice's eyes flitted around the room like she didn't know where she was. Her gaze passed over us all. Her attention returned to Stevie, and the temperature dropped ten degrees. Her eyebrows drew together, and Stevie turned to run.

The door slammed in his face. I held Stevie by the shoulders as he pulled at the door handle. "This is what you wanted," I said.

Larry called out to Stevie, and his voice seemed magnified. "You must talk to her."

Stevie sat crumpled in a ball by the door and held his head in his hands. "No! I changed my mind. I can't!"

I knelt by him. "You have to!"

Stevie looked into Alice's hate-filled eyes and tears gushed forth. "I didn't want you to be hurt," he wailed. "I lied to you. I was bad—horrible—but you were never supposed to be hurt."

The window began to rattle. The broken closet door slid across the room.

Larry raised his wand. The ribbons waved about the bronze rod as though a wind were blowing, but there was no breeze in the house. "Alice McGuiness!" he shouted. The window stopped rattling and the apparition turned its head to Larry. The mesmeric ribbons danced for Alice, and for a moment I thought it was over. For a moment, I thought Larry could talk sense into her.

But then she turned back to us, loomed over us, seeming to swell. The vessels in her throat bulged in a silent shriek, and the window shattered. Broken glass tore at the blinds and spun through and around Alice, reflecting fading window light like deadly glitter.

"Stop!" Larry commanded. He shielded his face and backed away from the spinning shards.

Alice raised her empty fist over us like it held a dagger. The temperature dropped yet again, and the glass cyclone backed us into a corner. The ribbons on Larry's wand shot forward. One of them entangled Alice's throat, and the other bound her arm. The spinning glass fell over the carpet.

When I had tried to grab Alice's hand the night before, my fingers passed through her, but Larry's ribbons not only touched her translucent body, they trapped her. With one free hand, the ghost pulled at the undulating ribbon around her throat.

"No!" Stevie shot up. "You're hurting her! Let her take me!" He tried to help Alice by pulling the ribbon around her neck, but the end of the ribbon reared up and hissed.

The flat ribbons plumped into living serpents. After seeing the house burning and the floor turning to glue, I thought this was another of the demon's tricks. Stevie relinquished the scaly bonds ensnaring his dead wife and fell on his ass, but Larry didn't seem surprised at all by the seemingly impossible transformation.

For the first time, Stevie met his dead wife's hateful gaze. She grimaced and snarled while trying to jerk free of the slithering serpents, but Stevie did not look away. She turned from his pitying gaze and fell to one invisible knee. Tears glistened in her eyes.

"I'm sorry," Stevie said. "What's going to happen to her?"

The sun fell below the horizon, leaving the room in darkness. Without the sun to overpower it, a pulsing light became visible in the closet. It throbbed like a heart, beating faster and brighter until the demon stepped out. The corner of his lip curled up as he looked us over. His ring emitted a brilliant flash of light. When our eyes readjusted to the darkness, Larry's snake ribbons writhed in the empty air where Alice's ghost had been trapped. Alice was gone.

"Impossible!" Larry shouted.

"Alice!" Stevie called.

The demon stood behind us. Larry swung his wand at him. Without moving his arms or legs, the demon circled around as quickly as Larry could swing. I dove at the demon, but passed through him as though he were a ghost, which I suppose he sort of was.

"Alice!" Stevie screamed again.

The demon cast his glowing eyes down at me as I lifted myself from the broken glass on the carpet under him. I'd been so focused on the spider ring, I'd never noticed the demon wore a Catalyst ring like Stevie's on his pinky.

Larry bashed the demon in the back of the head with his wand. There was no sound of contact, but the monster winced as though struck by a physical blow. The look of surprise on the demon's face was priceless. Something we did had finally affected him!

The entire room shifted, rotating a few degrees and tilting slightly. I had trouble standing, but Larry stood tall. I'd doubted him earlier, and thought him meek, but Larry now appeared to be in his element, far more potent than I had imagined. His snakes bound the demon as they had Alice, one around his neck and another around the hand with the ring. The demon grabbed at the snake around his hand, and the other one reared up and bit him in the face. He grimaced with pain and appeared to wilt. He fell to his knees, and I cheered.

The room shifted again. I felt myself sinking into the carpet, but Larry still stood firm.

Stevie crawled on the floor as though climbing a ladder. I remembered the smokeless flames and shouted, "It's not real!" But I couldn't take my own advice. No matter how I struggled, my limbs continued sinking into soft carpet like quicksand. Handfuls of carpet sank with me as I grabbed at it. The more I struggled, the quicker I sank, until only one shoulder, an elbow, and my head remained above the cold blackness. I reminded myself that the living room, not some dark abyss, lay below us on the first floor, but that didn't allay my terror.

A flock of shadowy birds tore through the shredded blinds and circled the room. I winced as the flapping shadows blew past my face, unable to use my hands to shield myself. Larry's snakes bit at the shadows as the birds tightened their circle around the combatants. They flapped between me and the demon and disappeared before orbiting back around, and along with them, the demon was gone as well. The snakes suddenly dropped again into lifeless ribbons. I felt foolish struggling on the now solid floor.

Stevie sat in a ball by the door. His hands and knees bled from crawling through the broken glass. "Alice," I heard through his sobs. "I'm sorry, Alice."

I looked to our expert to explain what had just happened.

Larry's arms fell to his side. "What the hell was that?"

CHAPTER 11

"What do you mean, *what the hell was that?*" I asked. "You are supposed to be the expert!"

Larry crouched to a sitting position on the carpet beside us. "I've faced some pretty powerful entities, but none of them could escape once bound by the Caduceus. I could hear Alice, but it was as though she were shouting over a great distance."

Stevie finally stopped sobbing and looked to Larry. "You heard her?"

"Yes."

"What was she saying?"

Larry looked to the window and the shredded blinds. "Ghosts aren't always all there. They get stuck in a frame of mind or emotional state, one obsessive thought repeating. They don't always know where they are or even that they are dead."

"What was she saying?" Stevie repeated.

"*I hate you,*" Larry said. "Over and over again."

Stevie just nodded his head and brought his knees up to his chin.

I groaned as I stood. "Could we maybe continue this talk downstairs, where there are built in lights?"

Larry nodded, and I grabbed his arm to help him up. Stevie remained in a sitting fetal position by the doorway. "Stevie?" I said.

He nodded and stood. We passed him, and he took another look at the bedroom before following us downstairs into the electric light.

Halfway down the steps, the doorbell rang, and we all froze. I slinked back into the bedroom and peeked out the tattered blinds. A police cruiser was parked behind my car on the street. I closed my eyes and inhaled the night air. Cheap aftershave greeted my nostrils, and I ran back to the stairs. "A cop! Decker!" I said. "The lights downstairs drew him right to us!"

Stevie's eyes grew wide.

"So what?" Larry mused. "Stevie still owns the house. We have every right—"

Before Larry finished the sentence, Stevie leapt over the banister. He landed hard, but rolled with the fall, crouching on all fours before rushing the sliding doors behind the kitchen.

Larry looked up at me, confused, and I pulled him with me as I rushed down the steps. "Stevie has the right idea!" I said. "If Decker finds us here, at best, he will arrest us for trespassing. At worst, he'll kill us and Catalyst will dispose of our bodies."

Larry gasped and hurried out the sliding door with me. We didn't bother to close it behind us. We followed Stevie, leaping the chain link fence into the neighbor's yard.

Death was a real possibility, but it wasn't the worst Catalyst could do. They might use us as guinea pigs in their twisted experiments. I'm sure they'd love to get their hands on me again.

"But…" Larry spoke between breaths. "I thought… Stevie is one of them."

A flashlight swept the backyard. We weren't being very stealthy the way we thumped around the house and slid open the door.

"He was," I said. "But then he came here with us!"

"Oh."

We were following Stevie, but it became obvious he had no plan. He ran blind. A dog started barking and the lights came on in a nearby house. Decker would know exactly where we were. Who would the neighbor believe: a bunch of disheveled trespassers or a policeman?

I sped ahead of Larry. Stevie was bigger and maybe even stronger than me. I'm not sure I could take him in a fair fight, but I tackled his legs from behind. Pebbles crunched as we slid.

"Stop!" I whispered.

Stevie kicked at me. "He'll kill us!"

"He will definitely kill us if we don't have a plan!" I shoved my car keys into Larry's chest and pointed left. "If you cut over that way, you should come out by the car. Meet me where the main street hooks into the subdivision."

"What about you?" Larry asked.

"I'll draw Decker away." The flashlight beamed around a house. "He's coming! Go!"

Larry looked reluctant, but once Stevie took off, he followed. A beautiful collie paced the yard next to me, running back and forth along the fence. Many would think he was angry, ready to defend his yard from strangers, but his tail was up and his eyes bright. He wanted to play. I crouched by the fence and he stopped to look at me, mouth wide and tongue lolling out the side of his mouth. We stared at each other.

Stevie and Larry weren't very stealthy. The flashlight swept in their direction. That's when I jumped up. My sudden movement startled my new friend. He jumped and twisted in the air, barking wildly. The flashlight swept back to me, and I met Decker's gaze. There was no point in trying to hide my identity. He knew my car. The dog barked and jumped while Decker and I sized each other up.

The back door to the house slid open and a young woman gasped. Decker looked her way, and I darted between houses. I could hear Decker running after me.

The collie continued barking, wanting to chase after us. I understood the dog's passion for the chase. The steady movement of my limbs and the cool night air in my lungs produced a feeling of euphoria. Since returning to civilization I'd gained a little doughnut of fat around my midsection from all the time sitting in cars, but I still had endurance. Decker was fast, but better suited to chasing a person in his cruiser than on foot. I imagined dropping my hands to the ground so I could race the wind like my dogs used to do, but my arms were much too short for running on all fours.

Somewhere in the distance, a familiar grinding made me wince. My car chugged and wheezed. They were flooding the engine! The starter on my Escort had some unique quirks if you weren't used to it.

I slowed down to give Decker a chance to catch up. I needed to distract him longer.

I stopped and listened. He wasn't behind me anymore, which meant he was returning to his car. "Shit!"

He could call for backup if he wanted to get us for trespassing or resisting arrest. Or, if he wanted to keep this private, he could just chase down my car. It wasn't like my wagon could outrace a police cruiser.

I listened for the grating squeak of my car engine and popped out from between houses just as it was speeding by. With a little luck, Decker hadn't reached his car yet. The wagon jerked to a stop, and I pulled at the rear door. It was locked! Larry reached back from the *passenger seat* and unlocked the door. Stevie was driving my car!

"What the hell, Larry!" I dove into the seat, and the car jerked into motion.

"I don't have my license," Larry said. "Believe me, it's a better idea to let Stevie drive."

I whipped out my phone. "This day can't get any worse."

The knot in my stomach relaxed a little when Diane answered. "Thank God you answered! I need to borrow your—"

"Jack," she said over the phone, "I'm kind of busy right now."

I heard a muffled voice in the background, something about turning in a report, and then Diane whispered, "I'm not asking him that."

"Is that Luis?" I said. "Are you still at work this late? I thought you were off?"

"No Jack, I'm not at work."

I thought about her in that dress last night and stopped breathing for a moment. "No!" I said. "Not Luis! He's your boss!"

"My jeep is in the regular parking space. You know where the spare keys are."

"I never said—"

"I know you, Jack. Is that all? You want me to check the dogs too?"

I took a deep breath. "Actually, could you take them to your place tonight?"

"In what? You'll have my jeep."

"I can drop them off. Assuming I'm not interrupting. I mean, you two aren't at your place or—"

"No!"

"At his place then?"

"We are eating out."

"Which restaurant? Is it nice?"

"Goodbye Jack." She hung up, and I sat in silence. It took a moment for the squeaking grind of my engine and the speeding landscape to come back into focus.

To date a coworker is bad enough, but her boss? That's the worst idea ever! What will happen when it goes bad? A worse scenario occurred to me. What if it *didn't* go bad? What if she married the creep? Luis was successful. He had money, cars, a vacation home… but he was an arrogant jerk. She could never be happy with a guy like him, could she?

"A little help?" Stevie said from the driver seat.

"Turn left up here," I said.

Stevie pulled into a Motel 6. I handed Larry a wad of cash and replaced Stevie in the driver's seat. "Get two rooms. If they ask for ID, use yours. No one knows you here."

"That could be a problem. My ID is still in my bag."

I slapped my forehead. "And your bag is still at Stevie's house!" If we were lucky, Decker was in chase mode and hadn't taken the time to search the house, but we hadn't been very lucky tonight. "Just get the rooms if you can. "If they give you trouble, ask to speak to Geeta Patel. She's the owner. Tell her it's for me. If you still can't get the rooms for some reason, just wait for me. I'll be right back."

My mind raced through a hundred scenarios. What could the cops, or worse, Catalyst, do with Larry's ID? Would Decker call out an APB on us, or would he want to keep this private? This was too big to handle alone. It was time to bring Luis in on it, but if I called now, Diane would think I was trying to interrupt their date again.

Diane's place wasn't far. I parked down the street and ran the rest of the way so they wouldn't find my car in her lot. A cop car crawled past, and I slowed to a casual walk. It continued down the street and disappeared around the corner.

It was a miracle Decker hadn't caught up to us.

I had a key to Diane's just like she had to mine, but I hadn't used it in over a year. Fluffy, her cat, rubbed against my leg and purred. I had watered Diane's plants and fed her cat while she was in the Caribbean with her sister. It was the only vacation she'd taken since I'd met her. Pictures of her Caribbean trip decorated a shelf. She looked happy, and I must say, although most might consider her rather plain, she looked good in a bikini top, her brown skin bronzed even darker by the tropical sun.

Plush pillows decorated the couch, making it impossible to sit without moving them first, but it looked nice. Everything was neat and tidy, nothing out of place. It smelled like dryer sheets, if that makes sense, not overpowering, not dirty, just… nice. I was suddenly ashamed at my own unkempt apartment. It was a wonder Diane could stand being in my mess, and she was there all the time helping with my dogs. I had helped Diane out that one time over a year ago, but she helped me all the time. I got the spare key to the jeep from a hook by the door and noticed a stack of Post-it notes and a pen on the counter. I didn't know what tomorrow might bring and wrote a simple message: *Not an accident.*

I loved driving Diane's jeep. It handled like a dream and drove off road better than anything, although Diane could never… NEVER find out I tried driving it off road.

My high school girlfriend had driven a jeep like that, an older model of course. Jessie had been so awesome. She'd even stuck by me after my dishonorable discharge, but when I disappeared for nine years, it made it kind of difficult to maintain a relationship.

I drove by my apartment to get the dogs but kept on driving. Decker sat in the parking lot, waiting. At this time of night, there weren't any other cars out. He saw me drive by, but didn't recognize the jeep.

The dogs had food and water. There was a pee pad in the apartment for emergencies, which was fine for Alpha, but Meega would give herself a bladder infection before she used it. They were still better off there than if I got killed or arrested.

CHAPTER 12

I was about ten minutes from the motel, but I turned onto the freeway instead. My brain felt full of mud. I needed to sleep in order to think clearly, but my thoughts and adrenal glands wouldn't let me relax.

How could Diane go for someone like Luis? He was just so… sleazy. She could do so much better. Luis spent more time farming work to other PI's than doing anything himself. I could count the number of cases he had worked since I hooked up with him on one hand. He was a figurehead, a face, more of a marketer than an investigator.

He was the first person people went to when they needed PI work because he had built a reputation and maintained that reputation. He had money, property. Maybe he wasn't so bad for Diane. He was certainly better off than me, with my tiny, messy apartment and a car held together with duct tape.

I almost missed my turn into the subdivision. I made my way very slowly, not turning down Stevie's street yet, just cruising by slowly. There were no flashing lights that I could see. I circled the subdivision and turned the jeep onto the drive. There were no cop cars, but the lights were now off downstairs, and I knew we hadn't stopped to turn them off.

I parked a few houses down and made my way to the house, scanning for people and cars as I walked. The street was quiet, all the houses dark. Hearing no movement in or around the house, I tried the front door and found it unlocked, just as we had left it.

Fortunately, it had not occurred to Decker to just lift the handle instead of ringing the bell.

I scanned the shadowy living room and found Larry's bag in the corner. There was no hint of cheap aftershave. Decker hadn't gone in the house and hadn't called in help. He probably didn't want the extra scrutiny. We might have caught a lucky break. It seemed Decker was going to keep this personal, at least for now. That way he could off me at any time without being officially involved.

Something tapped along the tiles in the kitchen. It got louder as it tapped closer, building in speed. My first thought was of Decker or another cop, but this was not a heavy human on two legs. Could it be the ghost or the demon manipulating matter along its path? My breath caught in my throat, and I pulled my gun from the shoulder holster.

A beautiful, wide-eyed collie tapped around the corner. His paws padded silently over the living room carpet. I dropped my arm and crouched to the floor, allowing the dog to run his warm tongue over my face. I let my legs slip from under me and sat on the floor with my new pal.

The tension eased from my shoulders while I patted him down, running my fingers through his thick fur. "How'd you get in here?"

A cool draft and the smell of lavender wafted in from the kitchen. We had left the sliding door open when we left. The nimble dog had jumped at least two fences to get here.

I blinked, and each time I closed my eyes, it was harder to open them again. This was the first time I'd sat still all day, and my exhaustion was catching up with me. I couldn't let myself fall asleep here. Larry and Stevie were still waiting on me.

Dogs don't grin, not really, but I could have sworn that's what the collie did when he closed his eyes and let me scratch behind his ears.

I stood, and, without a pause, the dog left the room, exited the sliding doors, and was gone. Normally, I'd escort the guy back to his yard to make sure he got home safely, but he seemed to know the lay of the neighborhood pretty well, and I didn't want the owner to report me to the cops. Decker would certainly intercept the call.

I missed my Meega and Alpha. I could relax if I had them with me and knew they were safe.

I hadn't heard anyone outside the front door. All I heard was the keys in the lock.

The newcomer didn't realize the door was already unlocked, so he actually locked it instead of unlocking it, which gave me extra time to slink into the kitchen. The sliding doors were still wide open, but I waited around the corner.

Dr. Ellison shoved his way noisily into the living room. Balanced on top of the two plastic tubs he carried was a portable light. No one that loud was trying to sneak up on me, but what would the doctor be doing here this time of night?

I crept silently out the rear sliding doors and circled back to the front door.

Dr. Ellison dropped one of the plastic tubs when I said his name.

"Mr. Mahler!" he said, clutching his chest. "What are you doing here?"

"I was watching the house," I said, which was not technically a lie. I had been watching it from inside. "May I come in?"

"Certainly."

And just like that, I went from trespasser to invited guest. Ellison flipped the light switch and cursed, "Blast! No power. I'll have to bring a generator."

Using *blast* as a curse word amused me. I could think of a few explanations how the power had gotten turned off since my last visit. The simplest was that the power company had turned it off, but with a rogue cop and a demonic ghost running around, it was hard to tell.

Ellison hadn't spotted Larry's bag in the corner and I was confident I could grab it without him noticing. Ellison may have been brilliant when it came to quantum particles, but not so observant of the people and things in front of him. He wore the same green sweater vest as I'd seen before. One side of his yellow shirt was untucked, but his clothes didn't smell dirty. I wondered if he had a closet full of identical shirts.

"What are you doing with all that equipment?" I asked.

His eyes were bloodshot, but he grinned with enthusiasm. "I haven't been able to stop thinking about what you said earlier today. Where did you see the ghost?"

"The bedroom," I said. "What is it that I said?"

He hauled a plastic tub upstairs, and I had to follow to hear his response. "If ghosts are real, maybe there are second chances." He was out of breath by the time he reached the bedroom. A cool draft blew in from the broken window, but Ellison didn't seem to notice. He expanded metal tripods and placed them around the room.

"Dr. Ellison," I said. "I still don't understand what you are doing here."

He twisted a copper wire around one of the tripods. "If ghosts are real, I should be able to contain them in an electromagnetic field. It's how we keep matter and antimatter separate in the Dynamo capsule."

A chill ran though me. "You can't do that."

He looked me in the eyes. "Why not?"

When I didn't answer right away, he continued spooling out the copper wire and coiling it around the tripods. This mixing of occult magic and science reminded me of something Catalyst would try, but that wasn't what bothered me most. If there was an afterlife, whether that was a heaven, hell, or something completely different, we didn't understand what it was or how it worked. If we trapped his daughter here, were we any better than that demon? We didn't understand enough to go meddling with people's souls.

"Listen," I said. "There is more going on here than I've told you. There is another entity." That got his attention. There was no way to sugarcoat this. "It seems to be keeping your daughter prisoner. I don't know what it is, or why it's doing what it is doing, but it is dangerous, not just for your daughter, but to living people as well. It can project images into our minds. I was in this house last night, and the building burned to ashes around me. I thought I was a dead man for sure."

Dr. Ellison looked around him, noting the obvious lack of damage.

I continued, "But when I got out of the house, the flames were gone, and the building still stood. Earlier tonight, the floor turned to mush." I pointed beneath his feet. "This time, I knew it wasn't real, but I still couldn't walk."

Ellison raised his eyebrows. "Fascinating! It was like you were living a nightmare! Did you ever experience a fire as a child?"

He still acted so detached. I got the feeling he enjoyed this mental exercise. "What does that have to do with anything?"

"I wonder if this *entity*, as you call it, is targeting your specific phobias or using common fears we all share."

I shook my head. "You aren't getting it! You are in danger every second you are here! This thing is dangerous and it is tormenting your daughter!"

"All the more reason to complete this EM field!" he said. "If I can't hold my daughter again, maybe I can trap the creature that's hurting her."

I didn't know what to say. Maybe he was right. Even Larry couldn't contain the demon. We needed something to give us an edge, but acting in ignorance could do more harm than good. We needed answers.

A breeze blew in through the broken window. The bedroom door slammed shut, and only Ellison's portable light illuminated the room. I waited for something to happen, some signal that we weren't alone. This time, it was just the wind.

"Maybe you're right," I said. "But I'm exhausted. I can't stay here with you tonight. Despite your enthusiasm, I can tell you're tired too. Do me a favor and wait until morning to try this. I have no reason to think the demon—"

"Demon?" Ellison repeated.

"—can't appear in the daytime, but at least you will be rested. Maybe by then, I'll have more information, and I can stop by and check on you."

He hesitated, looking back at his tripods and the spool of wire. His shoulders drooped forward. "Perhaps you are right."

We left his equipment, and I followed him downstairs. On the way out, I scooped up Larry's bag, and Ellison didn't even turn my direction. He was in his head, oblivious to his surroundings.

Ellison had to be one of the smartest men I'd ever met. Catalyst would love to recruit a guy like him. "Have you ever heard of Catalyst?" I asked.

"An agent which promotes change? Like heat or an enzyme?"

"In this case, an organization that promotes change."

Ellison shook his head. "No."

Ellison had no shame or worry about being here, no reason to be sneaky. I must have been in a daze earlier not to hear him pull into the driveway, mere feet from where I sat with the collie. I desperately needed sleep.

"Can you give me a lift around the corner?" I said.

He seemed to awaken from a trance. "Oh? Sure."

I got in the passenger side of his hybrid and directed him to the jeep. Ellison drove slowly, but it was faster than walking. He didn't ask why I'd parked so far away, so I didn't offer an explanation. I exited his car and said, "Do me a favor. Call me before you come to the house tomorrow."

"Oh. Certainly."

"Thanks." I shut the door and got in Diane's jeep. I let him pull away first, then made for the motel.

I checked in at the motel office first. The man at the counter didn't even ask my name, just handed me a room key. It paid to know people.

I halted at the top of the steps. An eagle perched on the rail in front of my assigned room gazing out at the parking lot. A breeze ruffled its feathers. I approached slowly, expecting it to leave as I neared, but it remained where it was. I'd never seen a bird that large outside of a zoo. If it stretched its wings out, it might be as wide as I am tall. It appeared dark brown in the parking lot lights, with pale gold curving over its neck and chest. Was this another waking dream?

Larry popped open the neighboring door when I opened mine. He must have been listening for me.

The bird lifted its wings and turned to face the motel. Larry flung the door wide, and stroked the bird's head. "What are you doing here?" He asked the bird as though expecting an answer.

"You recognize this eagle?" I asked.

"This is Dave," Larry said. "A friend of mine. He must have followed the bus all the way from Arizona." He let the bird perch on his forearm. "You must be exhausted!" Despite the bird's hollow bones, Larry still leaned to the side supporting the massive eagle's weight. "Ouch! Watch the nails, Dave!"

I was astonished, but, considering the other crazy events of the night, I was too exhausted to care much and was more interested in getting into my room and sleeping. Like I said before, Larry was in to some weird stuff. I shoved Larry's bag at him and the eagle snapped its beak in my direction.

"Jack's a friend," Larry said to the eagle as he took the bag.

"We caught a lucky break tonight," I said. "Stevie in there with you?"

Larry nodded.

"Did you have any trouble getting the rooms?"

Larry shook his head. "You must have made a real impression on the owner. Once the clerk called her, he just handed us the keys. Didn't ask for ID and let us pay in cash."

I smiled. I guess I'd done a good job for her. I'd taken some pictures of her ex-husband and his mistress. Hey, I never claimed my job was glamorous or noble. My pictures got Geeta out of a prenup and allowed her to keep this motel. On the downside, I wasn't welcome at the motel across town, still owned by her ex.

"I need some sleep," I said.

Larry nodded and brought the eagle into his room.

"You're taking the bird inside?"

"Just until morning," Larry said, shutting the door.

"Just don't let it make a mess!" I shouted through the door. "I know the owner!"

Imagining Stevie's reaction to the giant bird was amusing, but as much as I wanted to listen for it, I was too exhausted. I had planned on rooming with Larry, but if he was okay rooming with a criminal, I wasn't going to say anything. I hadn't been looking forward to sleeping in a patchouli cloud. That eagle would intimidate anyone wanting to do Larry harm in the night.

I washed my face and undid my hair. I lay on the bed flipping channels on an ancient television, thinking it would take a few minutes for the day's adrenaline to subside enough that I could fall asleep, but my eyes immediately became heavy, and I drifted to sleep with the Weather Channel quietly narrating tomorrow's highs.

CHAPTER 13

I tried to brush the wires off my head. My hair wasn't quite the buzz cut it had been in the army, but it was quite short. The fuzz on top reassured me that I wasn't as bald as I thought I was.

Dr. Bohman urged me to stop playing with the electrodes and continued with the questionnaire. His glasses reflected green light from the oscilloscope. He wasn't quite as plump as he had been the previous day. Questions popped up on a computer screen in front of me. I didn't read the words, but knew what they said.

"Do you enjoy working by yourself?"

"Do strong odors bother you?"

"Do you prefer being part of a team, or do you accomplish more on your own?"

"Do you replay conversations in your mind thinking about what you should have said differently?"

They were analyzing and categorizing my personality and aptitudes. Bohman's computer probably knew more about me than I did. I wondered if his computer found me docile and trainable and that's really why they had accepted me.

"If you were a tree, what kind of tree would you be?"

I didn't remember that question being on the test. This was odd and annoying, but I was desperate. Nobody wanted to hire a person with my record. I had tried joining the police academy, but they said they were full. I knew they weren't. As I pondered the possibilities, another question sprang before me.

"Where is Stevie McGuiness?"

Stevie McGuiness was in the room next door, but, no, that wasn't right. This interview had taken place over eleven years earlier. Stevie McGuiness would only be 16 years old. The computer was replaced by cards on a table. I flipped them over, one by one, revealing basic shapes. The last card repeated the computer's question. "Where is Stevie McGuiness?"

So odd to hear a computer refer to someone as *Stevie.*

"Mr. Mahler." Bohman glared at me under green glowing glasses. "You must answer the question."

The computer droned on, "Where is Stephen McGuiness?" *Stephen,* this time…

At Larry's first tap on the door, I shot into a sitting position. He was on his third knock before I fully remembered where I was. Bright light shone through gaps in the motel curtains, and the clock read 8:20 a.m. I didn't bother checking the peephole before opening the door. I'm not sure how I knew it was Larry. Maybe it was the gentleness of the knock or maybe, though I didn't notice it consciously, some of his patchouli fumes had crept under the door.

"Steve's gone," Larry said.

I didn't often remember my dreams, and the images had already begun to fade, but this brought it all back. So strange for Stevie to be the focus of a dream of my past. Maybe I should have turned Stevie in last night, but the cops didn't have any hard evidence against him. They would have released him… right into Decker's clutches. We weren't equipped to keep him prisoner, and he had joined us of his own free will.

"Let me get cleaned up," I said.

"Want to borrow a clean shirt?"

I looked at him for a moment. "No thanks." I'd worn uglier things than one of Larry's tunics, but I knew anything in that bag of his would reek of patchouli.

I let warm water stream over me in the shower, going over details and trying to decide where to start. The motel had little bottles of shampoo and conditioner which helped me work out some of the tangles from my hair.

I tied my hair back while it was still wet and flipped open my phone. Allen's phone went straight to voicemail, and I didn't leave a message.

We had travelled light, and Stevie hadn't left any clues where he might have run off to. He'd left his Catalyst ring on the table.

Larry had enough of my cash leftover for doughnuts and coffee.

Behind the coffee and patchouli, I sensed something else. "Did I dream it, or did you really have a bird in here?"

"Yeah. Dave ate a doughnut and then took off."

I raised my eyebrows, still not quite believing, while also wondering if that giant bird had scared off our skittish fugitive. "Eagles can eat doughnuts? Is that good for them?"

Larry shrugged. "He wanted one, but he just had a taste, then flapped off."

I instructed Larry to wait while I drove by my place. My poor dogs hadn't been out in sixteen hours!

Or had they? The door to my apartment hung open. The dogs were gone, but their food and water bowls were fresh. A faint wisp of Diane's perfume floated in the air. At first, this comforted me, but it wasn't the only foreign odor. On the bed sat a black and white photograph of old Abby dead on her kitchen floor. On top of this was a tiny syringe. I couldn't smell any leftover fluid on the tip of the syringe, but the implication was that its contents had killed Abby. I nearly jumped when my phone rang.

Decker's voice came deep and raspy. "Nice of your girlfriend to check on your dogs for you. Stupid of you to let her. I'd hate for her to have an accident like Alice or poor old Abigail Duncan. "

I chastised myself for not telling Diane I wasn't dropping off the dogs. I'd had so much going on in my head last night, and I didn't want to bother her again on her date.

"Where is she?" I asked. "Where are my dogs?"

"Relax," Decker drawled over the phone. "Your woman is fine."

"She's not my woman!" I spotted Decker at the gap in the stucco wall which led to the apartment courtyard.

He stared up at me with a wide grin, less than 100 feet away, but way out of reach. "You expect me to believe a cute girl drove your crappy car over at 2 a.m. to let your dogs out and she isn't your woman? Nice of you to protect her, but give me some credit."

Red scratches graced his face. I hadn't noticed those before. There was no point arguing.

"You see the package on the bed?" Decker continued. "That's evidence, see. You used that syringe to kill Abigail Duncan."

"You know that's not true!"

"Her death looked like natural causes, unless someone knows to look for the tiny puncture mark on her neck. If I don't say anything, no one looks for it, but I've got probable cause to search your place. If I find that syringe, the Medical Examiner finds the puncture, does a tox screen, and you're guilty of murder."

"I'll just destroy the syringe!"

"Like that is the actual syringe? You think I haven't done this before? The media will dig up your past in the military. No one will question your guilt."

A chill ran through me as I wondered how many others this man had killed by *natural causes*. "What do you want?"

"All we want is Stephen McGuiness. He's scum anyway. You don't need him. You don't even like him. We get him and we don't bother you again."

"What are you getting out of this?" I asked. "Is Catalyst paying you, or do you buy into that strongest survive bullshit?"

"Man has become weak and stupid. The world will be a better place when the strongest and the smartest take control."

"So they aren't even paying you?" That was bad. If there was a money trail, I could at least raise some reasonable doubt about Decker, maybe prove his involvement.

"That's none of your business. Bring Stephen to the top of the parking garage on Fifth and Cooper at 2 p.m. today. If you don't bring him to us, you'll spend the rest of your life in prison for the murder of Abigail Duncan."

With that, he flipped off the phone and marched around the building.

I raced down the stairs and narrowly avoided getting hit by a honking car as I darted across the divided street. The smell of aftershave got stronger as I circled the gas station. I panted heavily and stood over a puddle where condensation from his car's air conditioner had dripped onto an empty parking spot.

I thought losing my PI license was bad, but now I was looking at prison! Decker was right. With my past, no one would question my guilt. I'd already ruined my life once by protecting a jerk. Fool me twice, shame on me. I had to turn Stevie in by two, but I didn't *have* Stevie.

I walked back across the street and sped up when I saw my neighbor leaving his apartment. "Mr. Gibson!" I shouted.

The frumpy bald man tried to ignore me, but I blocked his path. "Mr. Gibson, did you hear anything at my place last night?"

Gibson scowled. "You mean like those unauthorized dogs of yours barking again?"

"Exactly!" I said. "What time was that?"

His eyebrows sank in the middle almost joining over his nose.

"Please!" I said. "This is important!"

"2:15 a.m.," he said. "You should know because that's when you left them out."

"It wasn't me," I said. "Someone picked the lock to my apartment!"

"Well, your dogs are safe at the pound this morning."

"You called Animal Welfare? Why didn't you just put them back in the apartment and shut the door?"

"That's not my business, sir. I'm not getting bit so you can keep pets in that tiny apartment."

"Alpha and Meega may make some noise, but they would never bite anyone!"

"Maybe. Maybe not," Gibson said. "They may be perfectly nice animals. You are the cruel one. Those dogs need space to run.

I can't imagine being cramped in a studio apartment all day. If you really cared about your dogs, you'd give them up."

With that, he pushed past and I let him go. All this time, I thought Gibson hated dogs. Turns out he hated the way I treated them. Perhaps he was right. Was I being selfish by keeping us all together? They were my family, and I didn't want to let them go.

I couldn't win this one. Maybe if I got the dogs back, we could run back up into the mountains together. I wouldn't need to worry about keeping my license, proving my innocence or paying bills. We'd have all the freedom we wanted.

But that wouldn't work anymore. Meega couldn't run with that leg of hers, and her teeth were worn down to nubs. She couldn't catch prey. There was no going back. Before I could do anything, I had to check on Diane. I locked my apartment, whipped out my phone, and made for the jeep.

A light voice answered the phone. "Hey, Jack. Where'd you end up last night?"

My heart thumped so rapidly. "Diane? Are you alright?"

"Why wouldn't I be?"

I closed my eyes and sank into the driver's seat. She had no idea of the danger she'd been in. "I'm coming to the office. This is too big. I need to bring Luis in on this one."

"He left town for a conference this morning."

"When will he be back?"

"Late Sunday night."

"Diane…"

"Yes?"

"I'm really glad you're okay."

She didn't seem to know what to think. "Alright."

I put the jeep in gear and drove three minutes to a big, brick building with no windows surrounded by chain-link fence. It reminded me of a prison. When I pulled into the big parking lot, the dashboard clock read 9:15. Office hours didn't start for another forty-five minutes, which is probably why no one had called me yet. We'd all been microchipped last time we were here, so they had my contact info. Fortunately, the door for pick up and drop off was open.

The smell of wet fur, urine, and Lysol greeted my nose before I even opened the door. I hesitated when I saw the man in blue coveralls at the counter. He chewed fruity gum and made notes on a clipboard. He didn't look up as I explained that my dogs had been picked up.

"If all their vaccinations are up to date," he said, "we'll just need to collect the $80 fee."

I gritted my teeth and whipped out my credit card.

He glanced at the card, then looked at his watch. "We can't take cards until the office opens. Someone will be here in forty minutes.

"I don't have forty minutes!"

He snapped his fruity bubble gum, still not looking up. "Well, then maybe you should watch your dogs better."

I took a deep breath. "You don't recognize me, do you?"

He looked at me for the first time. Even as disheveled as I was this morning, I was in much better shape than when he'd met me.

"I've been here before," I said.

His eyes grew wide, and the color slowly drained from his face. He backed away and made no move to stop me when I stepped behind the counter and made for the kennels. Dogs and cats shivered in steel cages. Some huddled in the rear of their cell. Others barked at me wildly.

Two and a half years ago, the man in blue coveralls had found me dirty and naked in one of these cages. I don't know how or why my body had changed on that particular day, but that's when I finally started the slow crawl back to humanity.

Catalyst viewed people like many viewed these animals. If you aren't one of the strongest or the smartest... If you can't or won't serve Catalyst's new world order... your life is disposable. Catalyst had explained to me how the weak and the stupid gain power, block progress, and keep people like me down. I had been kicked to the curb by society, stigmatized, unemployable... worthless. Catalyst had made me feel relevant and gave me purpose. Through their strange experiments, they had tried to make me strong. But their methods were as cruel as anything the *weak* and *stupid* masses had ever done.

My nose led me straight to Alpha and Meega. Alpha wagged his little bobbed tail and yipped at me. Meega, however, just lay in the back of her cage, staring at me. Her mouth bled where she had torn her gums chewing at the wire door. I pulled her out of the cage and stroked her while Alpha circled around us, his tiny tail vibrating with happiness at our reunion. At last, Meega gave my hand one small lick.

I marched out with the dogs following behind me.

The man in blue blocked our path. He stuttered as he spoke. "You can't take them." He was scared out of his mind, but he was trying to do his job.

I felt bad for him. "Who's going to stop us?"

He averted his eyes and moved away. He had my name now. I might have hell to pay later for this, but that was minor compared to getting arrested or getting killed while my family was imprisoned in here. The man in blue hadn't told anyone about the last time he found me here, and I hoped fear and embarrassment would keep him from reporting this occasion as well, but there was no guarantee.

I helped the dogs into the back of Diane's jeep. I never realized how thin Meega had become. She had gained a ton of weight when we started eating regularly, but all that was gone now. I'd switched her to wet food, but that wasn't enough. If we survived this, I'd take her to the vet.

I called Allen, hoping he'd pick up. I thought about going to the station and asking for him, but the fewer cops who saw us together, the better. I didn't want it getting back to Decker that I had a friend on the force.

"I'm not supposed to share leads," Allen said.

"There wouldn't be a case if not for me! The FBI hasn't even contacted me yet."

Allen hesitated. "They took the case, but they aren't doing much with it. They want to question Dr. Bohman, but they don't have a warrant or APB out."

"No warrant? Didn't they look at his files?"

"Listen, Jack, all you have on him, other than the fact he knocked you out and ran off, is a client list that happens to work at the same place."

"A place that does cutting edge energy research. They've had espionage cases at Sandia before. Someone tried to steal Ellison's prototype last year and—"

"Yes, but the only cases prosecuted were cases with solid evidence. If Bohman turns up, I can still bring him in for assault."

"What's the sentence on that— a small fine and he goes home?"

"It's all we have unless you dig up some better evidence." He added, "*Legally* dig up."

"One more thing," I said. "I think Decker is involved."

"Officer Decker?"

"Not so loud. Be careful who hears you."

"He's a cop, Jack. I might not always like his methods, but you've gone too far with this one."

I wanted to tell Allen about the threat and the fake evidence on my bed, but there was no point. It was clear he wouldn't believe me over Decker. "Just be careful," I said. "He's dangerous."

My heart felt like lead. How could Allen trust Decker over me? I respected Allen more than almost any other human I'd ever met, and I wanted so much for him to respect me too.

If no one was even looking for Dr. Bohman, he could be anywhere by now.

Anywhere.

Decker had said, *we want, we get, bring him to us.* I had assumed the *us* was Catalyst, but what if Dr. Bohman was still in town? It seemed ridiculous that he would stay, but so much of this didn't make sense. Why come here to steal energy research and then focus so much attention on Alice, a girl with no secret knowledge of her own. Her only value to the cause was her connection to her father.

With a little online snooping, I discovered Stevie had a sister and mother in Nebraska. The sister's listed phone was disconnected, and the mom didn't answer. I left photos of Stevie and Dr. Bohman with the ticket men at the train station, the bus station, and the baggage checkers at the airport. It paid to get in good with those people. They weren't at their posts all the time, but it was better than me trying to case all three places at once.

CHAPTER 14

I unlocked Diane's door, and Alpha rushed between my legs. Little Reece shouted with glee. Alpha circled the kid and wagged his tail. I didn't expect anyone to be here. Reece lay on the floor and giggled while Alpha covered his light brown face with warm kisses.

Meega slinked behind the couch. I'd never seen her not greet Reece. She was really upset.

Diane watched from the kitchen.

"Sorry," I said. "I should have knocked. I didn't think anyone was home."

Diane groaned. "The…" She paused. "Reece's dad dropped him off early." I knew Diane was about to say *jerk face*, but she never called her ex names in front of Reece. "He makes it impossible to plan. When the dogs weren't here last night, I went over to feed them."

I sank into the sofa. "I know. Thanks."

She sat next to me. "Are those the same wrinkled clothes you wore yesterday? What is going on, Jack? This was supposed to be a simple case."

I chuckled, and Diane and Reece both looked at me, surprised. Somehow, this made me laugh even harder, which made Reece laugh too. Tears filled my eyes before I was finally able to stop.

I took a deep breath and wiped my eyes. "Simple is not the word for this one."

"What's wrong with Meega?" Reece asked. The child lay on the floor behind the couch with the dog.

"She's mad at me," I said. "I've left her alone one too many times."

"Aw." Reece scratched Meega behind the ear, just the way she liked it. "Don't be mad." Meega gave the boy's hand one lick and then put her head back down. She was in full sulk mode.

"I've never seen Meega this upset," Diane said.

"They spent the morning in the pound," I said.

"The pound! They were fine when I left them!"

I put my hand on Diane's. "I know. Someone went in after you left. Someone involved in Alice 's death."

Diane's eyes widened. "Whoa! You weren't kidding about not being simple."

"I may have to go away for a while."

"What's going on?"

"I don't want you tangled up in this, Diane. There are some really dangerous people involved."

"If you tell me what's going on, I may be able to help. Give me a little more than a vague Post-it note to go on!"

I shook my head. "These are bad people, Diane. Whatever happens to me, promise me you won't look into it."

She brought her arm back and slugged me in the shoulder… hard.

"Ouch!"

"Don't play stupid man games with me, Jack! Tell me what's going on, and I'll decide what I'm going to look into and what I'm not."

I couldn't help but smile. "I know. That's why I… You are so awesome, Diane. I don't deserve you."

"What's that supposed to mean?"

"I don't deserve you being so nice to me."

"You're selling yourself a little short, Jack. I'm a good judge of character."

I looked at her skeptically. "Jerk Face and now Luis?"

She shook her head. "Shut up."

"Sorry."

"I don't see you dating any winners."

"That's true."

We sat quietly for a moment. Little Reece put out food and water for the dogs.

I finally found my words. "I wish you could see yourself through my eyes for a minute. You'd never settle for some jerk face again."

"I could say the same thing about you, Jack. Two years ago, you literally had nothing. Now look at you!"

Yes, look at me, I thought. *About to go to jail for murder.*

"Jack," Diane continued. "You are one of the good ones, always trying to do the right thing."

"No, I don't."

"You do!"

"Maybe when I was young and stupid."

"No, Jack. You never grew out of that, and I hope you never do."

I wondered what Diane would say if she knew I was trying to find Stevie so I could turn him over to the bad guys and then file my report as written, falsely labeling Alice's death an accident. "I've tried being the good guy before, Diane. Look where it got me."

"Sitting on the couch with me is that bad?"

I smiled despite myself, and gently tossed a pillow at her. "You know what I mean."

"You aren't going to tell me what's going on, are you?"

"I've tangled with some of these guys before. They scare me, Diane. The only thing that scares me more, is the thought of something bad happening to you or Reece."

"No one is an island, Jack. Everyone needs people they can talk to."

"You're a member of our pack, Diane."

"Oh, I am?"

"Yup! You, Reece, Alpha, Meega. You are my pack."

"And Luis?" she asked.

"He's just my boss."

CHAPTER 15

Ellison's car was already in the driveway when I pulled the wagon to the curb. It was pointless to keep driving Diane's jeep now that Decker had a bead on it.

The hood of Ellison's hybrid lay open. The door to the house was propped open by cables which connected to the car's engine. I called when we walked in, but there was no response. Larry and I followed the cables up the stairs and found Ellison working on his apparatus in the bedroom. He didn't look up until I introduced Larry.

"If you don't mind, I'd like Larry to stay with you while you are here. He has some experience with this sort of thing."

Ellison looked over his glasses at Larry. "Some kind of psychic medium?"

"Not exactly," Larry said. "Is this your ghost trap?"

Ellison looked down at the wires and poles which ringed the room. "I suppose that's as good a name for it as any."

"What about the top and bottom?"

"What do you mean?"

"Ghosts don't see the world as we do and they don't just walk along a horizontal plane. They move up and down as well."

Ellison raised his eyebrows. "I hadn't thought of that."

I snuck out while they were still talking. They would both be distracted for a while and they wouldn't be alone if the demon struck.

According to Stevie, there was another patient Bohman had been obsessed with for a time before losing interest and fixating on

Alice. Savory barbeque smoke rose above a house just a few miles from Ellison's. I felt like I'd been crisscrossing town for days.

When no one came to the door, I went around back and hollered over the wood privacy fence. "Mr. or Mrs. Dehwar?"

Conversation ceased. Four people, two couples, all turned to see me peeking over their fence. The man at the barbecue flipped a burger and said, "Yes."

"I'm sorry to bother you. I'm Jack Mahler, an investigator. I wondered if I could ask you a few questions privately."

One of the women shot Dehwar a glance of concern, and I knew it must be his wife.

Mr. Dehwar flattened the patties with his spatula, but never took his eyes off me. "Questions about what?"

"I'm investigating a doctor named Bohman. You knew him as Dr. Brown."

Mr. Dehwar nodded and handed off the spatula to his friend. "Meet me at the front door." Mr. and Mrs. Dehwar were already waiting with the door open when I got back around.

"You didn't seem surprised to hear I'm investigating Bohman."

Mr. Dehwar shook his head. "He's been cancelling appointments. For a time he insisted on seeing us three times a week, then he suddenly stopped. No one answers his office phone. Our prescriptions are almost out. What are you investigating Dr. Brown for?"

I shouldn't have said anything, but I did. "I suspect he's been manipulating scientists at Sandia Research Labs into revealing scientific secrets."

The Dehwars looked at each other, and Mrs. Dehwar said, "That doesn't apply to us. We weren't seeing him. We were taking our son there."

This threw my hypothesis out of whack. Their son had no more to do with energy secrets than Ellison's daughter. "So he never asked you questions about work? Never put a device on your head?"

Mrs. Dehwar almost smiled. "That silly contraption! No. But our son wore it during his sessions. We usually waited in the other room while they spoke."

"May I speak with your son?"

Mrs. Dehwar's mood suddenly darkened. "I'm not sure if he's awake."

"On a Saturday afternoon?"

"Sonny's medicated," Mr. Dehwar explained. "Our boy has problems. He has terrible nightmares and says inappropriate things. Child Protective Services started a file on us because of what he talked about at school. They thought he must have first-hand knowledge of the horrible situations he was describing."

"I would like to talk with your son if he's awake."

Mrs. Dehwar walked me into the child's bedroom while Mr. Dehwar went out to check the grill. I could have already told him the burgers had burned.

Sonny was a small child, much smaller than Reece. He wore footed pajamas and sat in a tiny chair next to the bed. Cartoons played on a small television, but Sonny stared at the wall. Hollow eyes filled half his head.

"Hello, Sonny," I said.

He turned his head and gazed at me for a time. "Are you real?"

"What do you mean?" I asked.

"Am I dreaming you?"

"I'm real," I said. "My name's Jack. I'd like to ask you some questions about Dr. Brown. Did you like Dr. Brown?"

Sonny raised an eyebrow and an intensity suddenly entered his eyes. "Mr. Mahler." He over-annunciated every syllable and for some reason it sent chills down my spine. "It has been a long time, but we remember you now."

"Who is *we*?" I asked.

"Always with the questions," the boy said. "It's nice to know some things remain unchanged. Your brain is different. We are having trouble getting inside, but we know where you are now. It is only a matter of time before we get you on our table and see what makes you tick."

"Dr. Bohman?" I said. "Is that you in there?"

A hand on my shoulder made me jump. Mrs. Dehwar looked down at me. "Sonny repeats things that he's seen and recombines them in strange ways."

The boy chuckled. "Why did you change when no one else did? We need more data, Mr. Mahler. It's not too late to join us. Only the strong will survive when Catalyst changes the world." Sonny scrunched up his face and turned away. "Mommy, I'm tired. I need one of my pills."

"Oh, honey," Mrs. Dehwar said. "We're running low on medicine. We need to save them for bedtime."

Sonny began to sob quietly to himself. "But I'm so tired."

Mrs. Dehwar embraced the boy with all her strength. A creaking step behind me alerted me that Mr. Dehwar had returned, and I left the room with him.

"Did he talk like that before you started taking him to Dr. Bohman?" I asked.

Dehwar let out a long sigh. "Yes."

I nodded, guessing what had happened. "And people were so disturbed because his words had some basis in reality. He spoke about things no child should know about."

Dehwar looked up at me with surprise. "Yes! You do understand!"

"Did he get any better after you started seeing Dr. Bohman?"

Dehwar nodded. "He slept better."

"Did he sleep better, or just more?"

"What do you mean? Is there a difference?"

"Can I see the pills Bohman had him on?"

Dehwar retrieved two medicine bottles from the medicine cabinet in the bathroom, and I read the labels. Galantamine and flunitrazepam, *for the treatment of sleeplessness.* A pill to make you remember and a pill to make you forget.

"We crush both pills into his juice thirty minutes before bedtime and then another of the white pills if he wakes up from a nightmare."

The white pill was the Flunitrazepam. "To help him forget the nightmare, I guess." But then why a pill to make him remember in the first place? "Did you get these at a pharmacy or—"

"Dr. Bohman gave them to us at his office."

I nodded my head. "I don't think you should give these to your son anymore."

"But he needs to sleep! You don't know what it was like when he would wake up screaming!"

"These pills don't do the things Bohman said they do. I'm not sure what they were for, to be honest. You need to get a new doctor."

CHAPTER 16

Sonny had something in common with Alice, but whatever it was, Bohman had lost interest in him. Alice had more of it or had it better. Dr. Bohman lived in a nice house on the same side of town. I did a drive by before I stopped. No one was watching the house, and there were no broken doors or yellow tape. The FBI wasn't taking this seriously at all!

The mailbox almost overflowed with envelopes and ads. No one had picked up the mail since he'd knocked me out in his office. The locks were nice, not easy to pick, and the doors and windows were rigged with alarms. Decker would be sure to intercept the call if I broke in.

Folded into the bulky pile of junk mail were a few bills: electric, water, Lazy Pines Rehab. It's a federal crime to read someone else's mail, kids. Don't do what I do.

Doctor Bohman had a sister in Lazy Pines, a nearby rehab facility! Perhaps that's why he wasn't leaving town right away. It was kind of sweet to think Dr. Bohman would risk getting caught for his sister, kind of humanized the twisted creep. I imagined what that big, greasy man's sister might be like— probably in a facility because her body couldn't support her own massive weight. Then another possibility occurred to me. What if she was in rehab because she was the subject of one of the mad doctor's experiments? That was closer to the profile I knew of Dr. Bohman. Imagine growing up alongside that evil psychologist!

I was forgetting my training. A good PI doesn't make judgments or assumptions. He gathers evidence.

Lazy Pines was a one story building, two hallways of patient rooms intersecting at a nurse's station and dining area. There appeared to be rooms for about 25 patients. I walked right in. Cleanser and feces filled the air. Instead of making it better, the cleanser just added another layer of stink. The nurse's station sat on my left, but I walked right. An orderly passed me, but I continued on, scanning the names on the doors as I went, and he didn't bother me.

One of the doors was propped open, and I caught a glimpse of a simple room. An old man sat alone clutching a string of rosary beads. A half-eaten tray of food sat on a table next to the bed.

A little ways down, people young and old spilled out of another room. It was nice seeing an old woman surrounded by loved ones. The woman's eyes silently cried out to me as I passed the doorway. "Grandma," I overheard. "You can't give my cousin the house! She wouldn't appreciate it! My baby girl needs a place—"

Another girl interrupted. "What about your jewelry, Grandma? If you don't put it in the will, Billy's just going to sell it off!"

A nurse with bright red hair, obviously dyed, stopped me as I continued down the hallway. "Who are you here for?" Gaudy red lipstick contrasted her pale, papery skin. It was the woman I'd seen emerging from Doctor Bohman's office yesterday! Her nametag read, *Cranston*.

"I'm looking for Elizabeth Bohman," I said.

The woman narrowed her eyes. "Betty doesn't get many visitors."

"Just her brother?" I said.

At that, her face reddened, and I could almost hear her heart beating faster. "You know Doctor Bohman?"

"We're old colleagues," I said, which wasn't technically a lie since we had been in Catalyst together. "He told me I might find him here."

Anxiety permeated her sweat glands. "He hasn't been here in days. If you aren't a friend of the patient, you need to leave."

"But I'd like to ask her—"

"Leave! Immediately. Unless you can prove some relationship to the patient, I will call the police."

Two large orderlies marched up to us.

"You can't prevent your patient from having visitors," I said.

"We will see what the police say. What answers were you hoping to get from a woman in a coma?"

One of the orderlies crossed his arms over his chest as they waited for my response. I'd been roughed up by much tougher guys than them, but there was no point in causing a scene. If Dr. Bohman's sister was in a coma, she couldn't talk, and I'd have smelled Bohman if he were here. I didn't need more trouble with the cops.

"Listen," I said, "I'm concerned about Doctor Bohman. No one has heard from him in a few days. I thought—"

"He's not been here," the nurse said.

Normally, I'd leave my card, but something told me Nurse Cranston wasn't going to be any assistance. "Okay. Thanks for your help." They followed me to the door, and Nurse Cranston whipped out her phone as I left.

The sky outside took on a yellow hue, and the wind stopped blowing. I felt like I had walked into a still photo. If this change in atmosphere had happened back in the Midwest, I would have expected a storm to be coming, possibly even a tornado.

I opened my car and Meega shot out the door past me. She landed hard on the pavement. I hated to think what that would do to her bad leg, but she kept running. She must have slipped out the door at Diane's and somehow snuck in the car when I wasn't looking. She could be pretty quiet, but she'd never done that before. I'd never seen Meega so upset with me. I'd freed her from the pound and immediately abandoned her again.

Meega never let her rear right leg hit the ground, but she maintained a good pace, skipping over the parking lot and heading right into the highway. Traffic wasn't busy this time of day, but it would only take one car to kill my dog. I couldn't believe what I was seeing. Ever since she'd been hit, Meega avoided cars like the plague. She even stopped and looked both ways before crossing a street. Something had either terrified her, or she was intentionally committing suicide.

I left my car door hanging open and raced for the road. Meega slid past a moving car and I lost sight of her until she emerged and rounded another.

Moving headlights barely registered. When I looked up, a semi sped straight for me. On top of the trailer, a green cape billowed in the wind. The demon smiled down at me. It was surreal, seeing him in daylight under a bright yellow sky, standing confidently with his hands folded atop the racing semi.

I stepped out of the semi's path. Tires squealed and a horn blared as I ran into a moving car and bounced into the air. The demon and the semi dissolved into nothing. The sky returned to its normal blue and I fell in slow motion through the gentle breeze. Before I could fully appreciate the atmospheric change, my back and head came to a sudden stop on hard asphalt.

CHAPTER 17

My ears rang. Somewhere in the distance I heard a female voice. "…Hell… What were you doing?" Puffy white clouds floated in the sky above. I blinked and slowly moved my head. The movement was stiff and made my head throb.

"Don't try to move," another woman said. Nurse Cranston shone a tiny pen light in my eye.

The first woman again: "He ran right into the road. I swerved and tried to stop, but there wasn't time. Is he a patient or something?"

The thought of me being a patient at Lazy Pines amused me. I wasn't an old man. But then, if I had broken my back on the road, maybe I *would* be admitted to this place. Maybe that was the plan, to get me back in Bohman's clutches. He could experiment on me at will, and I'd have no way to run.

A man's voice: "How is he?" Officer Allen's concerned face floated above me, and I smiled. This is how Meega must have felt when she got hit two years ago.

"He's probably got a concussion," Cranston said. "He was lucky. They'll do a CT scan at Lovelace Medical to look for bleeding and skull fractures."

I didn't have time for hospitals. I shot into a sitting position and immediately regretted it. I felt like I'd left part of my head on the road, but when I touched my hair, everything was intact. The world looked slightly skewed. Allen's car, an older Crown Victoria with flashing red and blue lights, blocked the right lane. His cruiser almost looked antiquated compared to Decker's Charger.

I had almost made it back to the sidewalk before I'd gotten hit, but I was still in the road. The woman who hit me had indeed slowed down. That was the screeching I'd heard. If she hadn't, I might not be alive at all.

Allen put a firm hand on my shoulder. "Easy. This is your second bump on the head in as many days. They say you walked right out into traffic. What got into you Mahler?"

I stared into Allen's face for a moment. "Meega," I finally said.

"Your dog? Is he around here somewhere?"

"She," I corrected.

Cranston brought her hands to her hips. "He's confused. Head injuries will do that."

I wondered if Meega had really been there. I didn't smell her anywhere, but that didn't mean anything. The semi had dissolved, not real. For some reason I hadn't expected the demon man would appear in broad daylight. I couldn't trust anything I was seeing. Was this really Officer Allen? He smelled like Allen. I grabbed Allen's shoulder, and he supported me while I stood.

One of the drivers stuck behind Allen's car applauded. I'm not sure if he was genuinely happy for me or being sarcastic, and I really didn't care. I reached for my phone. The screen was cracked. With effort, I brought the numbers into focus. It was 2:05 and I had one missed call. It would take fifteen minutes to drive to the rendezvous with Decker. "I'm late!"

Cranston said, "You're not going anywhere! The ambulance is less than a minute away."

"I've got aspirin in the car," I said.

"A great idea," Cranston said. "If you have a brain bleed, that will make it worse. If you need pain relief, we've got acetaminophen, but you need to be evaluated by a doctor."

I glared at Cranston. "Why would you care?"

Allen's mouth hung open, and he shot an apologetic glance at Cranston. "This nurse from Lazy Pines called 911 and has been looking after you while we've been waiting for the ambulance. I wouldn't be here if she hadn't called it in. You might try *Thank you.*"

"It's my duty to help," Cranston said. "Even bastards who harass my patients."

"You're helping Bohman," I said. "I know it."

"Of course I am. His sister is a patient."

A car horn blared in the background. The sound felt like an ice pick stabbing me through my temple.

"You know where he is," I said. "Don't you?"

She gave me a half smile. "Dr. Bohman is a great scientist. All he wants to do is help people. Stop harassing him and his family!"

"Help people?" I repeated. "Are we talking about the same guy?"

Allen raised his hands between us. "It's okay," Allen said to Cranston. "I'll watch him until the ambulance arrives. Thank you for your help."

Cranston lit a cigarette and sucked in the nicotine on her short walk across the parking lot. It always surprised me to see healthcare workers light up.

"Bohman's a *federal* case now, Mahler. What's your deal?"

"The FBI may not be interested in him stealing energy research, but he is still involved in Alice McGuiness' death."

Allen raised his hands again. "You have some proof?"

I opened my mouth and immediately closed it again.

Allen shook his head.

I put my hand on Allen's shoulder and looked deeply into his eyes. "Allen, there are only three human beings in this world whose opinion matters to me."

I didn't know what else to say, so I made for my car. Allen called after me, but I ignored him, and he made no effort to come after me. Traffic was already thinning out now that I wasn't blocking the road, but it still took forever for a friendly driver to stop so I could exit the parking lot.

I know it wasn't safe, but I checked my voicemail as I raced west on I-40. I expected to hear Decker saying he was releasing his fake evidence, but it was my contact at the bus station. Stevie had purchased a bus ticket to Nebraska. His bus would leave at 3:15. The bus station was only five minutes from the parking garage. There was still time to pick him up before it left, but how long would that take? I'm sure he wasn't waiting out in the open, and I was already ten minutes late for the meeting with Decker, but wouldn't Decker be happier if I was late and had what he wanted?

Screw that! I couldn't let another person suffer for my freedom, even a jerk like Stevie. I'd meet Decker alone and take the consequences. For all I knew, he'd already released his forged evidence. Maybe I'd get a few good licks in before he arrested me.

At least I'd finally have that time off from work I'd longed for. Diane would make sure the dogs were okay. She'd probably find them a better home than mine, and they'd all be better off.

Three meals a day on the state's dime wouldn't be so bad. I'd been through much worse.

Winding my way up the parking garage made me dizzier than it should. I felt nauseous by the time I reached the top. Nurse Cranston might have been right. I could really have gotten a concussion. There were no events at the stadium today, so there were only a couple cars on the lower level of the garage. The sun beat down on the deserted upper level, and I parked near the stairwell.

I got out, but quickly dropped behind the car. A bullet split the cinderblock just above my head. I peeked over the hood of the car to see Decker taking aim. The security cameras were all pointed down slope and away from us.

"That silencer's not police issue," I shouted. "What gives? I thought you were going to frame me, not kill me."

He stalked closer with gun and eyes aimed straight ahead. Soon he'd have a clear shot and the car wouldn't be any protection. "New orders."

I wondered if that were true or if he had planned to kill me all along. "I know where Stevie is!" I called out, desperate to buy time, but Decker didn't stop.

I ran for the stairs and heard a bullet dig into the wagon's fender. I was glad I was using my own car again. Diane would have killed me if I had returned her jeep with bullet holes in it.

"What did my car ever do to you?" I shouted as I dove into the stairwell. The effort made me dizzy again. I held the metal rail to steady myself as I climbed down the stairs and out of Decker's direct line of sight. I was a sitting duck, but he didn't enter the stairwell after me. Decker didn't realize I wasn't operating at 100%. He was going to box me in down at the exit. If he couldn't shoot me now, he'd arrest me when I left and shoot me down the road where there were no witnesses or cameras.

This morning, Stephen had been Decker's priority, but now he was intent on killing me and didn't give a crap where Stevie was. Something must have changed, but what? I remained as ignorant as I had been when he threatened to frame me this morning.

I hated to do it, but I needed to call for help. I whipped open the phone and asked Allen to come down to the parking garage. "I need you down here right away!"

"What for?" he asked.

"It's a matter of life and death," I said. "Mine!"

He sighed. Allen never seemed to get excited or anxious, no matter what I said. "Alright. I'll be right there."

I stayed where I was. At least here I could hear Decker coming from above or below.

At last I heard Allen blare his siren. I peeked over the edge of the garage. He was talking to Decker. I got in my car and headed out the gate. I waved at Decker as I drove past him. He couldn't take me in or shoot me with another cop watching, though I half expected him to try. He supposedly had that fake evidence, but all he did was glare at me. A little ways down the street, I pulled over and texted Allen: *Thanks. You literally saved my life.*

My investigation had evidently touched a nerve to get Decker so riled up.

CHAPTER 18

The blare of the bus horn stabbed into my head. I was in no mood for subtlety and parked my wagon at the exit lane in front of the bus. I boarded the bus before security could react. The driver yelled, but a quick scan was all it took to see Stevie wasn't on this one.

"I'm a PI," I said. "I've got reason to believe a dangerous fugitive is boarding a bus to Nebraska."

"We're going to Nevada!" The driver shouted. "Get that car out of the way!"

I got off and met Stevie's eyes as he lined up for the bus behind this one. Luggage sat in a line on the curb, but Stevie only had one bag slung around his shoulder. He took off, but I was already running, and tackled him to the ground.

"You idiot!" I said. "You think Nebraska isn't the first place they'll look! You want to put your mom and sister in danger?"

"How do you know about—?"

"Decker's less than a mile from here. They're going to call this in, and he'll be here before you can blink. I suggest you come with me."

"Damn you!"

Security surrounded us, but Stevie said, "It's okay. I'm going with him."

We made for the wagon amid suspicious looks from security and passengers alike.

Once in the wagon, I pulled away from the honking bus, and downtown transitioned into strip malls.

"Did Alice ever have dreams that came true?" I asked. "Or reveal things that she shouldn't have known?"

"Sometimes, I guess."

I was low on patience. "You guess?"

"She used to ask about things that happened to me on the job, things she shouldn't have known. She referenced little in-jokes we had at work. For a while, I thought one of my coworkers was spying on me for her. When she started asking about my meetings with Dr. Bohman, I started to get concerned, but she never pieced together what we were talking about."

"Did she ever dream about the demon man?"

Stevie shook his head. "She used to have really bad nightmares, but she didn't talk about them. Alice stopped remembering her dreams after she started her sessions with Bohman."

I nodded. "A drug to make you remember and a drug to make you forget."

"Huh?"

"I'm not sure. Just thinking out loud."

Strip malls gave way to housing additions and Stevie asked, "Why are we going back to Rio Rancho? Won't Catalyst be watching the house?"

"They think you left. I've got friends there looking for answers, but we won't stay long."

Stevie saw the cables leading from the hybrid car into the open front door of his former home. "What the hell are they doing?"

I didn't feel the need to answer. My head pounded, and I was still pissed off. As soon as we walked in the door, the light in the house gained a shady blue tint as though a cloud of Midwestern fall leaves blew in front of all the windows at once.

"Larry?" I called. "Doc?"

Larry appeared at the top of the stairs. "Steve! Of course, that makes sense. Something started happening as soon as Steve walked in. Quickly, get up to the bedroom!" He ran past us and started Doc Ellison's car.

Stevie hesitated, but I pushed him forward, and he didn't resist. Halfway up the steps, the stairs flattened into a slide. I grabbed the banister and caught Stevie with my other hand before we had the chance to slip too far. It had to be another of the demon's illusions, but I wondered how an illusion could make us fall down like that. I guess our eyes determined where we planted our feet.

Stevie managed to crawl past me up the steps, and I followed close behind. He reached the top of the stairs, but when I put my hand on the top floor, the stairs completely collapsed, leaving me hanging by my fingertips over a deep, dark chasm. I wasn't sure what would happen if I let go. Would I fall somewhere, or just float in empty space because I really crawled on solid stairs? I was too afraid to find out, at least by choice. My sweaty fingers ached as they clenched the top step.

I'd already experienced how illusory peril could mask real danger. That's how I got hit by that car. Real or not, pain shot through my fingers and my arms quaked. I couldn't hold on much longer. The up side was that I forgot all about my headache. The power cables dangled beside me. I thought about using them to haul myself up, but I'd likely yank something loose and destroy whatever Doc had planned when the danger to me wasn't even real.

Stevie grabbed one of my arms and tried to pull me up, but I was too afraid to let go of the ledge and let him help me. A hand pushed on my back, and my chest toppled forward onto the top floor leaving my legs lying on perfectly normal stairs. Stevie still grasped my arm with both hands. Larry stood on the step below me with his hand on my back.

"What are you stopping here for?" Larry said, running past us. "The trap is in the bedroom! We may only get one chance at this."

The bedroom only lay a short distance down the hall, but the hallway elongated, stretching further and further. Larry had already passed us into the room, seemingly a mile away, but I kept bumping into the wall.

I closed my eyes and held my head. My nose found the smell of fresh paint somewhere ahead— the paint they had used to cover the bullet hole in the bedroom wall. I extended my hand, found Stevie's wrist, and pulled us forward, following the scent.

"What took you so long?" Larry asked.

I opened my eyes to find Larry just within the doorway and Doc in front of the window. The tripods circled the room and there was now a metal plate suspended on the ceiling.

Stevie halted in the doorway when he saw his father-in-law. Ellison's brow furrowed and his fist clenched.

Before they could confront one another, the room darkened, and day suddenly turned to night. The remaining half of the closet door rattled. Alice shot out of the closet surrounded by bubbles. I imagined hearing a splash. Her hair floated in the thickened air as though she dove under a surface of water. The bottom of Alice's red dress trailed up and behind her as she reached for her wide-eyed husband.

Doctor Ellison gasped. His hand rested on some kind of lever. Alice hovered in the middle of the room, not far from the metal plate on the ceiling.

I called out to Doc Ellison, "Wait!"

Doc froze, looking to me for some explanation, but I wasn't sure why I had said it. Maybe I was being superstitious. I still didn't like the idea of trapping Alice's soul, or ghost or whatever she was, but if we weren't going to try, what was the point of all this?

Before we could have a theological debate, clawed fingers closed around Alice's torso. The fingers appeared giant at first, but then it was Alice who was small. I hadn't seen her retreat, but she was suddenly at the closet entrance again. The demon tossed her like a discarded soda can into the darkness of the closet behind him and scanned the room with his orange eyes.

He regarded Larry suspiciously for a moment. I knew the Caduceus had to be in the room somewhere, but Larry wasn't holding it. It was the only object I'd seen capable of hurting the monster. When the demon saw Stevie, he blurred to the center of the room and opened his mouth into a wide, shark-toothed snarl. His neck thickened, and his jaw detached like a snake. Lips stretched the full width of the demon's head, and saliva dripped from rows of teeth which lined the path down into the monster's body.

Stevie froze against the wall, and I could see it wasn't by choice. The wall had sprouted hands the same color and texture of the painted drywall. They bound Stevie tightly, and an arm locked around his neck.

I wondered what would happen if the demon swallowed Stevie. Would that be an illusion too, or would the monster suck Stevie's soul down into whatever hell Alice was trapped in?

Doc stared in wide-eyed amazement with his hand still on the lever.

"Pull the switch!" I shouted, but he didn't seem to hear. "Doctor Ellison!"

Doc jerked to attention and pulled. The air snapped, and ozone stung my nostrils. The sun shone brightly outside the window, and Stevie fell forward onto the floor. He sucked in quick gulps of air, but remained physically unharmed. The demon was gone. Larry crossed the center of the room to look after Stevie. If there was really a force field in the room, it didn't appear to impede living things or solid objects.

Doc stared at the spot where the demon man had been. He still held his hand on the switch. "That was the thing holding my daughter?"

"Yes," I said.

Doc shook his head, suddenly angry. "I don't understand! The electromagnetic bubble was supposed to trap him."

"Maybe he's in there." I waved my hand around the middle of the room. "Just invisible. Maybe your bubble cut him off from the rest of the room and that's why everything went back to normal."

"No," Larry said. "He's gone."

After all that, we still weren't any closer to defeating the monster or finding the truth. Stevie brought his breathing back under control. Ellison gave his son-in-law a single disgusted look and began testing his cables with some sort of voltage meter.

What was I missing? Decker had tried to kill me. He must think I'm on the verge of some breakthrough, but perhaps he was giving me too much credit.

A distant siren chirped, putting me on high alert. "Decker!" No one moved. They hadn't heard it. I tugged Stevie up by the arm. "Decker's almost here! We've got to scoot!"

Stevie snapped to attention. "He's coming?"

I directed Ellison and Larry, "Stay here. He's got no reason to come after you. He only wants us." I hoped it was true. Hurting Ellison would certainly bring Decker unwanted attention.

By the time Stevie and I were downstairs, the unmistakable growl of Decker's car had reached the driveway. With the front door propped open by cables, he could walk right in.

I led Stevie out the back and we peeked around the corner of the house. Decker had parked in front of the driveway, blocking Ellison's car. Once I was sure Decker was in the house, we made our way for the wagon.

"And you made fun of me for parking down the street," I said.

Stevie shook his head. "How did you know he was coming?"

"He blew his siren at the corner to stop traffic so he could make the turn quicker. This wasn't a random drive by. Someone told him we were here."

"Ellison?"

"No."

"Not Larry?"

I cranked the engine and looked over my shoulder to make sure Decker wasn't running out of the house. There was no way we could outrun his car. He'd knock us right off the road with that nudge bar.

"Not one of us," I said.

"But the only other people there were…"

"Ghosts."

CHAPTER 19

Nurse Cranston was the only new variable I could think of. She lived in a two bedroom ranch. I rang the doorbell and detected the faint smell of the greasy doctor. "Doctor Bohman's been staying here!"

Stevie became crazed. He started banging on the door. "Let us in, Bohman!"

"Relax!" I looked over my shoulder to see if anyone was watching. "He's not here now. No one's home."

Stevie kicked the door, leaving dents where his boot hit the wood. There were easier ways to get inside, if that's what he wanted to do, but a dam of pent up fury had burst within him. Blood vessels on his temple throbbed as his face reddened and he kicked again and again.

"I'm not a cop," I said. "I'm not authorized to break in!"

Through gritted teeth, Stevie said, "You're not the one breaking in!"

He had a point. *Plausible deniability.* I *had* tried to stop him.

The doorframe couldn't stand up to Stevie's beating, and finally slammed inward. Stevie leaned against the frame, panting.

"Feel better?" I asked. Pushing my way past him, a wall of stale cigarettes hit me. A stack of mail lay on the dining room table. It didn't look like she'd used the table to eat on in quite some time. If it were cleaned off and de-cluttered, it would look really classy.

Bohman's greasy smell centered on the guest room and an unmade bed, but there were no clothes or possessions, nothing to clue me in to his plans or whereabouts.

"Damn."

Pictures of Cranston and a slender man decorated a shelf in the master bedroom. Clean men's clothes hung in the master closet alongside Nurse Cranston's clothing. Dirty scrubs stunk up the hamper, but the smell was barely detectable amid the acrid, stale, tobacco.

Stevie sat in the living room with his head in his hands. "He's not here."

"Nope. He slept here, but he's not coming back."

"How can you be sure?"

I flipped through the stack of bills. "He took all his stuff." An envelope caught my eye. The return address was Lazy Pines. Why should Cranston be getting a bill from her employer? I threw it on the floor next to Stevie. "Open this."

"Why?"

"Plausible deniability."

He shrugged and tore open the letter.

I immediately snatched it away. The bill was for a patient named Carl Cranston, with almost the same list of medications and supplies as the bill for Bohman's sister.

"There are no dirty men's clothes in the hamper…" I said. *"… A great scientist. All he wants to do is help people… "*

Stevie's mouth hung open. "Huh?"

"I *had* gotten close. Cranston's helping Bohman because he claims he can help her husband, but he's lying." I took a deep breath of cigarette-tainted air. "I think I understand now. We've got to get to Lazy Pines before it's too late!"

CHAPTER 20

I called Larry, Doc Ellison and Allen en route, but I didn't want them there until I'd gotten the lay of the land. An ambulance idled at the main entrance to Lazy Pines, and I feared we were too late. The rear door of the ambulance hung open, but the back was empty.

I shoved the doors of Lazy Pines inward with a little too much force, but the time for subtlety was over. Orderlies wheeled a gurney toward the door at our backs.

Cranston tried to bar our way, but without talking or breaking stride, I rushed around her left while Stevie sped by her right. The woman on the gurney had buzzed, sandy-blonde hair and glowing LED lights implanted at three points into her skull. Her cheeks sank inward and her jaw hung open, but she was still recognizable.

Stevie grabbed the patient's limp hand. "Alice?"

Alice's eyes flicked back and forth behind her eyelids.

"I'm calling the police!" Cranston said.

"Good!" I shouted. "Please do! This isn't who you think it is! This isn't Bohman's sister!"

I almost missed the greasy scent behind us. Bohman stood in the hallway with a suitcase in his hand. He stared at us, frozen with shock, then suddenly dropped the case and bolted down the hall. I started after him, but one of the orderlies grabbed me. He let go when Stevie punched him in the face. I felt bad leaving Stevie to deal with the two orderlies, but I couldn't let Bohman slip out the back door.

The mad doctor looked back and saw me catching up to him. He darted into a patient's room, what had been Alice's room, and I had him cornered. An IV hung next to the bed. Doc must have needed something more potent than pills to keep Alice comatose full time. Sunlight streaked in from the blinds. Bohman panted, and sweat covered his pudgy face. Even that short run had worn him down.

"It's not too late," Bohman said, trying to catch his breath. "You are strong, clever. You should be one of our foot-soldiers, marching society forward."

I shook my head. "Terrorism is not moving forward!"

"Terrorists?" He almost laughed. "Why use explosions when we can use media and politicians to spread chaos? Why get our hands dirty when a well-timed internet meme causes the masses to bring down modern institutions for us? We are already taking over, Mr. Mahler. Future generations will edify us as saviors!"

"Do your masters even know what you are doing here? You were sent to gather energy secrets, and you were good at it. No one suspected what you were up to until you kidnapped Alice McGuiness. What were you doing to her?"

He sneered. "Even our great and glorious leader can be shortsighted. He underestimates the potential power of the human mind. You remain like the rest of the sheep, Mr. Mahler, standing in the way of progress. When the great cataclysm comes, and we rise to take our place, you will die with the rest of the unworthy."

Bohman rotated the stun ring on his finger. He'd zapped me with it before, but now that I knew what it was, there was no way I'd let him get it close enough to use it. He was no match for me physically. To my surprise, Bohman brought the ring to his own neck and jerked rigid. He slid down the wall and landed face up on the floor.

"What the hell?"

A cloud passed over the sun outside, casting the room in pale blue. An eerie mist oozed from Bohman's mouth and clung to the floor around him. He seemed to be mouthing words. On closer inspection, long, narrow cylinders poked up from behind his teeth. I thought they might be large worms at first, but they were tipped with fingernails. Hands stretched Bohman's lips wider than should be possible without tearing skin. The demon smiled at me from within Bohman's mouth. His white hair slicked backward as Bohman's face gave birth. Once his head was free, the demon's hair rebounded into the familiar devil-horn crest. He rested for a moment, legs still impossibly hidden somewhere within Bohman's unconscious body, and stared at me with those orange eyes before twisting completely free and hovering over the prostrate scientist.

Mist poured out of Bohman's mouth like vaporous afterbirth. Everything the mist touched twisted slightly, taking on an evil, threatening countenance. The legs of the creaking bed curved inward. The mattress sank in the middle, and green stains diffused over the fabric. Mildew grew up the sides of the walls.

I backed away from the horrific site and bumped into Nurse Cranston. "What the hell is that?" She rasped.

"I think that's how Doctor Bohman sees himself in his mind... or rather... how Doctor Bohman sees himself in *Alice's* mind. We have to wake Alice up!"

Cranston called after me as I ran. A woman in one of the patient rooms shrieked in mortal terror. It was the old woman I had seen with her family that morning. I was initially comforted to see that her family was still with her now, but my relief was misplaced. The old woman twisted and fell from the bed, screaming again. She crawled for the door, but was missing an arm from the elbow down. Alarms buzzed at the nurse's station.

One of the old woman's family members skipped out of the room carrying a bloodless arm. Another family member, a daughter, I think, hovered over the old woman with a hatchet. I grabbed at the woman with the hatchet, but my hands passed through her like a shadow.

The old woman continued to wail on the ground as her family hacked off bloodless pieces and divvied them out among one another. I couldn't touch her attackers, but I l knew how real the demon's illusions could feel.

There was nothing I could do for the old woman here.

I left the horror, but stumbled when another patient's doorway exploded in a ball of fire. Flaming residue fell on the tiles outside the room. Within, a bed sat on a rocky outcrop hovering over a river of lava. Young boys with red skin and horns hung from the walls and prodded the patient with tiny pitchforks. The old man clung to the bed frame, crying and shaking his head as the devil children tried to nudge him off the bed and into the lava below. It was as though Bohman's illusions were leaking out and indiscriminately attacking everyone around him.

Cranston's eyes reflected orange light from the lava. "Father Dempsey? We have to help him!"

I was already up and away. "That's just a distraction! The only way to help them is to get to Alice!"

Stevie still wrestled with the two orderlies. The demon rose behind Alice's gurney. My breath stopped for a moment. I shook Alice, trying to wake her. She moaned. The demon flickered and wavered, but Alice couldn't wake up, and the monster continued to grow, swelling to the height of the hallway.

The metal rail of the gurney twisted around my arm, trapping me as the demon loomed larger. He rested one bent knee on the tiled floor while his hair bumped the ceiling. His spider ring twitched its mandibles above my head.

Adrenaline shot through my system, and I suddenly fell free, hitting the floor ass first. Whatever my arm had really gotten caught on must have finally given way. I rolled away from the snapping mandibles. When I rose to my feet again, the demon had disappeared, but I knew he wasn't gone.

"Adrenaline!" it suddenly occurred to me. An injectable form of adrenaline, or epinephrine, was used to treat severe allergic reactions and heart attacks. Lazy Pines had to have some somewhere. "Cranston!" I shouted over the moaning patients and beeping alarms. "Epinephrine! We need to wake Alice up!"

Cranston came forward wielding a syringe in her hand, but froze in her tracks. I followed her gaze and saw a slender man in a yellowed, faded suit. His face was also faded, just as it had been in Cranston's photographs back at the house. The shade extended his arms to the nurse as though waiting for a hug.

"He can still do it." Cranston's arms dropped to her sides. "Bohman can bring Carl back to me."

"It's not real!" I shouted. "Everything Bohman says is a lie. Everything he shows you is an illusion!"

Cranston shook her head, and tears dripped from her eyes. "It can't *all* be a lie." She motioned toward the mirage. "He's right there!"

I grabbed the syringe from Cranston, but caught movement through the corner of my eye. Meega stood over Alice, legs planted firmly on the gurney. She growled and barked. Foam dripped from her worn canines. I'd only ever seen her like this when she was defending me. I reached forward, and she snapped at my hand. She'd crack her leg if she jumped off the gurney without help.

"Come on, Meega," I said. "This isn't you." I didn't know why I was talking to her. She couldn't be real, could she? She smelled real this time. Had Bohman somehow lured her here? Could he affect the minds of animals as well as humans? Meega'd done so much for me, and I'd done nothing but hurt her. I was never home with her, and I'd gotten her picked up by the pound again.

But I had gotten her off the streets. She'd have never survived as a stray with those worn down teeth and broken leg. I'd had her leg taken care of, and she had Alpha to keep her company when I was away. Diane and I took her on walks, so apartment life wasn't as bad as it could be. She no longer had the energy to run free like we used to and didn't need as much activity. She adored Reece, and Reece adored her. We were still a pack. She might seem better off with someone else, but she didn't *trust* anyone else. She trusted me.

I smiled at her, and she cocked her head as though confused. I cautiously moved my hand forward palm up. Meega snapped her jaws half-heartedly, but did not connect, and I continued forward while the counterfeit dog watched. I brought the syringe down into Alice's thigh and pushed the plunger.

Alice scrunched up her nose and moved her head, but she did not awaken. Meega ignored me as I shook Alice. "Wake up!"

Alice's eyelids shot open, revealing tiny, glowing moons. She snapped her jaws, and massive canines jerked up at me. I fell back. "Alice?"

Her muscles twisted, and she arched her back while howling with pain. Meega was gone now, forgotten, but Alice barked. This physical transformation didn't seem possible, but I'd seen what Catalyst was capable of. They'd done it to me. It was so similar to my own nightmare. Was my subconscious feeding another illusion, or had Alice's reality influenced my dream?

A shadow sprang up behind me. The demon's fingers sprouted and branched like sharpened tree roots, leaving me trapped between two monsters.

"Alice!" I shouted. "Wake up!"

The sneer plastered to the demon's lips faded and his brow wrinkled with concern as he looked past me.

"Honey?" Stevie held Alice by the shoulders. She was a sleeping woman again. The wolf was gone, and I let out a sigh of relief. Tears dripped from Stevie's eyes.

Without moving a limb, the demon receded from me and swelled behind Stevie. The monster's lips grimaced in an inaudible hiss. His arms closed in around Stevie but halted before touching him.

Stevie grabbed onto his wife and clenched his eyes shut, blocking all distraction and danger from his sight. "Alice! Wake up!"

Alice moaned, and the sun peeked through the front entranceway. The demon recoiled from the light and shrank to normal size, appearing as real and solid as any man. He watched from the shadows, gritting his teeth. I rushed to Stevie's side and grabbed Alice's hand. Alice looked up at me, then at Stevie, confused.

Stevie smiled, still crying. "Oh, Alice," he said. "It's going to be better from now on. I've lied to you. I betrayed you, but I'm different now."

The demonic man shriveled like a deflating balloon. Recognition dawned over Alice's eyes as she looked up at her husband. The demon brought his tiny green cape over his shrunken face.

Alice's voice came out a hoarse whisper. "Get away from me."

Stevie shook his head. "I love you, Alice. Things will be—"

Alice cleared her throat and her hand balled into a fist. "Get away from me!" She slugged Stevie in the chin.

The demon collapsed into shadows and was dispelled by the clear fluorescent lights. Alice's effort exhausted her, causing her to fall into a daze once again.

Doc Ellison ran in with Larry a few steps behind. Doc glared at Stevie and embraced his daughter. "Alice!" he said. "You're alive! You're okay!"

I let go of her hand and shook my head. "I don't know if I'd say she's *okay* exactly."

Ellison rocked his daughter in his arms. She didn't respond, but he talked to her anyway. "I'm leaving the Dynamo project. I've given enough of my life to science. My next project is my relationship with my daughter."

Larry wielded the Caduceus, but the ribbons hung limp, dormant. "That's why we couldn't trap the demon. He was never really inside our bubble. His image was being projected from here, from Alice's mind. When we turned on the bubble, we blocked him out instead of trapping him in. Bohman had no power of his own. He was enhancing and manipulating Alice's natural abilities"

I nodded, speculating. "The drug cocktail must have primed her mind and sharpened her experiences, but it left her unable to remember what Bohman was doing so she couldn't fight back."

Stevie held his chin. Alice's weak punch hadn't done any physical damage, but there was no mistaking the hurt in his eyes. "She's got to understand. Things can be different!"

I stepped between him and Alice and locked his eyes with mine. "She doesn't *got* to do anything. Your whole relationship was a lie from beginning to end."

"We can begin again," he said.

I shook my head. "You helped me out on this, Stevie, and you helped Alice in the end. I owe you, and I know better than most how Catalyst can get into your head. The cops don't know your part in all this yet. When they do, you'll be a wanted man, and Catalyst is already gunning for you. You want my advice?"

Stevie stared blankly at me.

"Go while you still can."

Stevie looked past me at his wife. "But—"

"Life as you knew it is over. You'll live the rest of your life on the run, or you'll live the rest of your life in prison. The choice is yours."

Stevie looked at me one last time, then down at his wife. He marched out the door, right past Allen in his policeman's uniform. Allen had no idea who Stevie was or that he was involved in any of this as they crossed paths. I'd told Stevie a small lie. There was no clear evidence to implicate him. There was enough suspicion to launch an investigation, but Catalyst was good at covering its tracks.

Lazy Pines remained in chaos. Orderlies confined patients to their beds while nurses tried to revive patients in cardiac arrest.

"Mahler!" Allen called. "What's going on here?"

"Kidnapping," I said. "I may never be able to prove Bohman was stealing energy secrets, but this..." I pointed at Alice on the gurney. I didn't have any evidence against Decker either, no cashed checks, nothing. I hated to think he could get off scot-free. I'd tell the authorities about poor old Abby, but there was no guarantee they could tie it back to Decker. I'm not sure how much longer I'd survive in this town with him gunning for me.

I led Allen to the room where Bohman was waking up. I pried and twisted the copper ring off Bohman's pudgy finger and presented it to Allen. "See: stun ring."

Allen ignored me and cuffed Bohman's hands behind his back.

CHAPTER 21

I took a long, meandering way home and found myself on that same road where they had found Alice's car. They would dig up her grave and find some other woman buried there, another victim of Catalyst, Doctor Bohman, or Decker. She had most likely been dead long before the car hit that tree. The accident had pulverized her face, and the morticians put it back to match Alice's photo as best they could. No one questioned that it wasn't perfect.

Police lights flashed red and blue ahead, and smoke rose from the same tree where they'd found Alice's doppelganger. I slowed down and pulled in behind the dodge charger. Decker's car had planted its nudge bar halfway into the tree with the front end of the car crumpled like a soda can. Though he was trapped within the crushed metal frame, Decker still breathed. The air bag had deployed. They built those cars to take a beating.

Maybe I should have been happy seeing him like that after all the pain he'd caused others, but I couldn't enjoy the grisly sight. I couldn't imagine what had caused him to drive into the tree at such speed, but it got him out of my hair for the moment. I thought of driving away, but I called the accident in to 911 and waited.

Once the police and paramedics arrived, I made a quick statement about how I found the car and left.

I had dogs to take care of.

I was surprised to spot Alice in the apartment parking lot when I took the dogs out for their morning walk Monday. She was already looking full and healthy and wearing her favorite dress again. Even her hair looked thicker. I figured she must be there to thank me. I led the dogs down the stairs, but Alice was gone when I rounded the last steps.

Before going to the office, I took a detour and stopped at Doc Ellison's. The house smelled of toast and coffee, and Ellison was wearing a green apron over his ochre shirt.

He greeted me with a smile. "Alice just woke up. She wants to meet you."

I followed him into the spare room and found Alice sitting up in bed, nibbling from the tray which straddled her lap. Her face was pink and alive, but she was still underweight. Darkened LED lights peeked out from a layer of stubble, but her hair would soon completely cover them.

She smiled when I came in. "I dreamed about you this morning."

"Did you?" I asked.

"You were walking your dogs."

I nodded. "Did you also dream about Decker?"

She sank into the bed. "The policeman."

I nodded. Whatever Bohman had done to Alice, it had permanently changed her. She'd never be easy prey again.

Doc shooed me away from the bed. "Alice needs her rest."

Alice grabbed my arm. "I've been sleeping for weeks. Stay for breakfast."

"I've got to go in to the office," I said. "But I want to check in on you again tomorrow. Maybe we could have breakfast then. Would that be okay?"

She nodded. "Of course. If not for you, Mr. Mahler, I'd still be lying in that hospital bed, or moved to a facility out of town somewhere where no one would have ever found me."

I smiled. "Just doing my job. After all the things I've seen, it's nice to have a happy ending once in a while."

"You've been in some dark places, haven't you, Mr. Mahler?"

"I have."

"But you're still a bright person."

"I don't know about that."

"No, you are. How do you do it?"

I shrugged. "I'll visit again tomorrow."

Before leaving, Ellison grabbed my hand in both of his. I was afraid he was going to hug me, but he didn't go that far. "You've brought my daughter back to me. Now, it's up to me. You've given me a second chance."

I nodded. "You've gotten off to a good start, but it's all still fresh. As time moves on, it will be difficult to keep up this kind of effort."

"I'll do it. There is nothing more important than my daughter."

CHAPTER 22

I didn't know why, but the scent of tobacco and bourbon at Luis's office annoyed me. Diane beamed when I walked in. I was ready for Luis to lay into me for being late, but he grabbed me by the cheeks and slipped a cigar into my shirt pocket. "There he is! The star!"

I would never smoke the cigar, but I might sniff it later. I'd never seen Luis so happy. He was practically giddy.

"You did good, Jack! Real good! Net Life is thrilled with us. They can't pay out a policy on someone who isn't even dead! They're coming to us for all their casework in the state from now on!"

Luis had his hand on my back and led me to the conference room. "You've already got another big client lined up. You're going to love this, Jack! An old friend asked for you specifically."

The door swung into a cloud of cigar smoke and bourbon, and my heart froze. A man with an open suit jacket rested one leg on the conference table. His blond hair was buzzed in military style, and he held a glass in one hand.

"Hey, Jackie!" Anderson said. "Been a long time. You're really making a name for yourself out here."

I hated when he added an -ie to my name like that— so disrespectful! "What do you want, Sergeant Anderson?"

"Not a Sergeant anymore. I went private. Lots more money in it. I want to hire you, Jack. I need detecting, and my old buddy's a detective."

"I'm not your buddy, and you know that."

I marched out and Luis followed me. "Hold up, Jack. What's that all about? He's got the biggest case that ever walked in that door! I thought you'd be thrilled to be working with an old friend."

"He's no friend. He's the reason I got kicked out of the military. Everything bad that's happened to me over the last eleven years can be traced back to that guy."

"We're talking big money here, Jack!"

"Then give the case to someone else."

"He doesn't want anyone else. He only wants you. At least hear what he has to say. It'll only take a few minutes to hear him out. What have you got to lose?"

I shook my head. "Famous last words."

ABOUT THE AUTHOR

Matthew Barron spends his days mixing and analyzing human blood as a medical technologist in Indianapolis, Indiana. Matthew's diverse fiction has appeared in magazines and anthologies such as *Ill-Considered Expeditions, Roboterotica, Outposts of Beyond, Sci Phi Journal, House of Horror* and more. He's produced two of his plays and released three graphic novels: *Temple of Secrets, The Brute* and *Harmony Unbound*. His sword sorcery book, *Valora*; dystopian novella, *Secular City Limits*; and kids book, *The Lonely Princess* are also available.

Photo by Liz A. Thomson

For more information, visit
matthewbarron.com
or
submatterpress.com